I0719922

HUNTING MALICE

ALSO BY ALEXANDRA RYDER

Silent Borders

HUNTING MALICE

ALEXANDRA RYDER

A THRILLER

CHAPTER 1

The moon cast an eerie glow over the desolate streets as if nature conspired to amplify the sinister aura surrounding me. I moved through the city like a predator searching for prey, my senses attuned to the dark longing coursing through my veins. Ahead, my next victim emerged from his car and began striding toward the front door, oblivious to the danger lurking in the darkness behind him.

Following is an easy, natural part of the hunt. I'm alone, unseen, and ready to slide closer, careful and quiet, a silent spectre lurking within the dancing shadows. The only sound that broke the unsettling silence was the whispering rub of the rope I'd looped tightly around his throat, depriving him of thought and air.

"Not a sound," I hissed in a chilling whisper, my voice barely audible. "Do exactly as I say, or I'll slit your throat. Do you understand?"

He nodded stiffly, his face increasingly dark from the lack of air. With a controlled pull on the noose, I allowed him to taste the suffocating fear, providing him just enough hope to keep him docile and compliant. Time was of the essence.

I swiftly immobilized him with tape, ensuring his readiness for what awaited him.

The empty house beckoned, its windows bathed in the ethereal glow of moonlight while a tropical breeze whispered through the air. A growing pressure surged within me, a powerful and intoxicating sensation yearning to be unleashed.

I turned to gaze upon my victim as the initial flicker of fear transformed into a raging inferno of terror within his eyes. In that moment of connection, our gazes locked, pulsating with a twisted understanding fueled by his racing blood and impending agony.

A cacophony of wild music surged within my inner ears, each note resonating with the imminent climax that lay ahead. The sound of the knife piercing his skin reverberated through the empty house, its impact growing into a final chorus of fulfillment and exultation.

Tonight, I stood as his judge, ready to extract retribution for the sins that stained his soul.

CHAPTER 2

I listened to the tranquil waves gently lapping against the shore as the wind tousled my hair. The sea stretched before me; a mesmerizing shade of blue mirrored the vast sky above while the sailboats danced across the horizon like delicate butterflies in an artful masterpiece. It was a place of enchantment, or so I wanted desperately to believe, until the jarring sound of my cellphone chiming broke the spell. I glanced at the screen: dispatch—a new case, another life extinguished.

With a sense of urgency, I navigated through the intermittent gaps in traffic and jogged toward the nearby parking lot. The address provided by dispatch led me to the prestigious Upper East Side of Miami. When I got to the crime scene, a crowd had huddled by the gate. Several reporters were circulating through the crowd, hungry for pieces of information. I stared for several minutes at the onlookers, wondering if someone in the crowd knew something. For all I knew, one of them could be the killer.

Quite a bit of traffic was going by while more curious people arrived. The house where the murder occurred was waterfront with an unobstructed canal view, a few miles to Aventura Mall, and a short boat ride to the Intracoastal and Haulover Cut for ocean access—no security cameras in sight.

I showed my badge to one of the uniforms at the barrier and strode up the distance to the front door. As I stepped inside, I noticed how shocked my team's faces were. Cops face daily gruesome and brutal things, but they have learned to hide their feelings in the presence of death. And yet, whatever they had seen was so horrific that they couldn't control their emotions.

A sense of unease crept up my spine. The body of an older man was hanging from the ceiling, his face set in a tight mask of agony, presumably caused by a knife slamming through living skin and bone into his body. His genitals had been removed, and his torso's skin had been stripped and draped around his arms to resemble wings. Hooks were bored into the ceiling, and ropes held up the body. His legs were held together with tape. The stench of fear and despair hung heavy in the air, a haunting reminder of the evil unfolding here.

For a few seconds, it didn't seem necessary to breathe. I just stared. It reminded me of the Viking "Bloodeagle" ritual, a form of punishment and execution; the graphic ritual method sees the victim's back sliced open, their ribs severed from the spine with a sharp tool, and their lungs pulled through the opening to create a pair of "wings" while still alive.

My trained instincts kicked into high gear as I observed the meticulous precision with which the crime had been executed. The mutilated body, grotesquely displayed like a twisted work of art, sent chills through my body. The scene bore the chilling signature of a sadistic psychopath who derived perverse pleasure from inflicting pain and suffering on their victims.

"This one is special, isn't it?" said Philippe Balu, the lab forensic, peering over my shoulder. "I hope for him that he was already dead when the killer did that to him."

Not according to the Viking ritual, I thought.

"This has yet to be confirmed," I said instead.

There was a quiet rush of air, and I looked beyond Philippe to see that Sergeant Tony Moretti had arrived. He glanced around the room, and I was waiting to see his reaction to something this extreme. He stared at the body for several seconds, cleared his throat, and beckoned me to come closer.

"Well, Detective Olsen, as an ex-special agent for the FBI, what can you tell me?" he asked.

I felt a bit of irony in his voice, as I felt every time he mentioned my work at the FBI, but I pretended not to notice. I decided not to mention the similarity with the Viking "Bloodeagle." Maybe my imagination was too much fed by the legends of my grandparents, who were originally from Norway.

"This isn't a spontaneous kill," I answered him. "The crime was planned ahead of time."

"What makes you think that?"

"It takes time to mutilate a body like this. The knife wounds are precise and very deep. It has been a slow, deliberate killing performed with great accuracy. The killer is a professional in butchering people. Which means a sadistic psychopath."

"If this is his signature, we have never had anything like it in Miami."

"It doesn't have to be the same pattern. We need to examine the unresolved cases to see if they have something in common with this one. Maybe the killer was trying to find his signature."

"That's a very ... interesting thought, Detective. But I still believe that our best bet is to find a witness. Maybe somebody saw something. So, let's concentrate on that for now."

He patted my arm and walked away toward the medical examiner, who estimated that death had occurred on Monday, the previous night, around eleven o'clock.

I looked at the body again, but there was nothing else to tell me more than I already knew. I turned away from the body and stared around the room, and that's when I felt like I was missing something. But what?

As I watched Tom Bishop, the blood spatter analyst, taking a blood sample, I got my answer: there was too much blood. No human being had such a large volume of blood in his body, which meant that some of the blood belonged to someone else.

Could it be the killer's blood? I intended to ask Tom how quickly he would do the blood analysis when our phones buzzed—we received a match from the facial recognition system.

According to the system, the victim was Harry Miller, the head of Sunshine Build Group, one of the largest construction companies in Miami, specializing in design, construction, and high-end remodeling. The house belonged to the company.

Moretti crossed the room, clearing his throat to get our attention.

"All right," he roared, eyes turning to him as if they were on the same switch. "Now that we know the victim's identity, we will follow standard procedure: Officer Sanchez and I will notify the family. Detectives Olsen and Freeman will search for possible witnesses. Detective Bennett will check the neighbourhood for security cameras. I want everyone at headquarters by five o'clock. Questions?"

There weren't any questions.

"Okay," concluded Moretti. "Let's get to it."

After Moretti and Maria Sanchez walked out the front

door, I joined Detective John Freeman. We had been partners for almost six months, and we seemed to understand and support each other reflexively. John was African American, around five-eleven, built like a chunk of granite, with facial features to match. He was married to a beautiful Cuban woman and had a three-year-old son.

He told me he'd spent the last twenty minutes canvassing the neighbourhood and looking for security camera footage.

"Any luck?" I asked.

"Not enough to say hello to the killer."

"Let's see if we are luckier with the neighbours," I said.

The first possible witnesses were an elderly couple who lived in the house next door, to the left. They were shocked that such a violent crime had taken place in their neighbourhood, but they had not seen or heard anything suspicious.

Same with the other neighbours. It should not have been much of a surprise. Sometimes, people are so afraid that they hide information that could help the investigation.

Disappointed, we headed back to headquarters, hoping that the forensic experts would have some answers for us.

CHAPTER 3

Judging by the number of northern license plates, many people had come down to enjoy the warm, sunny weather at the beach. Driving among those happy tourists on this perfectly sunny day felt odd while trying to catch those lurking in the shadows.

Back at headquarters, I poured myself a coffee and followed the team into the conference room. Usually, Moretti gave everyone enough time to get ahead with the case before holding the meeting. I was wondering if anyone had any leads at this time.

"Let's get started," he said.

He briefed the information officers on what they could and could not release to the press and then asked for reports on the progress in finding the killer. Everybody gave him a brief rundown, and he listened impatiently, looking at us expectantly.

As I'd thought, there wasn't much. We had nothing except two footprints of different sizes that did not match in the system. Meaning there were two killers. The forensic technicians were waiting to hear back from the labs. Moretti's frustration was visible when he realized we had no relevant evidence to point us in a specific direction.

"Come on, people, this is a vicious crime," he said, his voice holding more than a smidgeon of irritation. "I need you to find something. Officer Wang, were you able to confirm the chain of command at Sunshine Build Group?"

Lee Wang, the crime analyst, cleared his throat. "Yes, Sergeant. Miller's son, Jeff, will take over as CEO."

"There you go," Moretti exclaimed. "That's motive."

"I don't know, Sergeant," intervened Maria Sanchez. "The guy seemed pretty broken up over his father's death."

"If he'd killed him, would you expect Jeff Miller to show up happy?" asked Moretti.

"No. Of course not," Maria answered.

Moretti let the silence grow while glancing around the room to ensure everyone followed the conversation.

"Sorry," he finally said, "remind me how many murders you've worked on again, Officer Sanchez?"

Maria looked utterly flustered. "This will be my first."

"Right," said Moretti, an ironic smile on his lips. "That's what I thought."

Maria's mouth opened for a moment, then closed. She had decided that it was wiser to keep her mouth shut.

"Officer Wang, what do we know about the victim's personal life so far?" asked Moretti, ignoring Maria's discomfort.

"Well, um, he was extravagant," answered Wang. "He collected expensive cars, houses, and boats. Not necessarily in that order."

"Married?"

"Yes. And divorced once."

"What was his relationship like with his ex?"

"You realize, Sergeant, that I started working on this case an hour ago!" Lee said, his jaw clenched in frustration.

"What's your point?" asked Moretti.

"I'll look into it," replied Wang, realizing it was pointless to upset Moretti.

"Thank you."

"There is something else," Lee added. "The Sunshine Build Group has a ninety-million-dollar contract pending."

"That's another motive: competition," exclaimed Moretti. "Our job is to ensure that his death had nothing to do with the impending deal. It is also necessary to check the company's stock. Did it take a hit? Something like this can be expected when the head of one company is murdered. This means we should look for anyone who sold or shorted the stock before his death. That's what we call motive."

He deflected anyone from possibly adding something, leaving no room for doubt that he was in charge.

"To verify all you have mentioned," John said, "we need access to certain people's phone records, emails, and bank accounts. You have to try to get us warrants."

Everyone agreed with him.

"You guys are nuts! " replied Moretti. "There's no way to get them. People always hide things in companies that play with millions of dollars. But they also have connections in high places. No judge will give me those warrants."

"We know that," John said.

"You know that, but you still want me to waste my time trying?"

"Yes," said John. "The fact that Miami has never seen such heinous crimes must convince the judges. We will make sure the suspects know we will investigate anyone who sold or shorted the stock before his death. Hopefully, they'll grant us access if they have nothing to hide."

"And if one doesn't?"

"They become the focus of our investigation."

Moretti didn't have time to answer. His phone started buzzing, and he looked at it impatiently. We watched his face as he listened, then frowned deeply.

"Oh, Jesus," he said. "We have another body. Dispatch will send you the GPS coordinates."

Ten minutes later, John and I were slaloming between vehicles in traffic. The sun was still bright in the sky when we arrived at the crime scene, which was as disturbing as others. The killer dumped the body of a young woman behind a canopy of bushes bordering the courtyard of a large apartment building on Jackson Street. The building was five stories high and had two wings.

"I'll check for cameras," John said.

"I can see two cameras from here," I said. "Hopefully, they're angled right."

"Hopefully," said John while moving away.

I scanned the body head to toe. The things that the killer had done to what had once been an attractive young woman were best left unseen. The knife wounds were precise and deep, similar to those on Harry Miller's body. Could there be a connection between the two murders, or was it my imagination?

I wanted to know if I was the only one who thought of this, so I stepped over to where Tom Bishop was poking at some eventual evidence.

"Hey, Tom. What've you got?" I asked him.

"Not much. But take a look. Did you notice anything familiar about the stabbing?"

"I did. The wounds are precise and very deep, like the ones on Harry Miller's body," I explained. "And there is no blood because the killer committed the crime elsewhere."

"What else?"

"There was too much blood at Harry Miller's crime scene, meaning some of the blood belonged to someone else. Could it be her blood?"

"Great job! Liv Olsen, you're a hell of a cop."

"I don't want to interrupt such a chummy scene," John said. "But I need to talk to Liv."

Tom raised his eyebrows. "Of course, Detective Freeman," he said jokingly.

I followed John, ducking under the yellow tape and stepping away from the crowd.

"What do you want, John?" I asked him.

He turned around and faced me.

"There are four cameras around the buildings, but they last worked some time ago. And, according to the administrator, two hundred forty people are living here."

"And we have to question every one of them," I said, discouraged. "We're going to need a workforce."

"Yeah, I know. It's shaping up to be a very long day. But there is something that can help us get a lead."

"And what would that be?"

"I think I know the victim."

"Not sure?"

"Ninety percent. I've only seen her once, but I know someone who can confirm whether I'm right."

"And who is this someone?"

"He's a friend of mine. I can call him, and if he is available, we can meet him and show him the victim's photo."

"It will do little good. The facial recognition system will tell us who she was in the next few minutes."

"I know that. But my friend may know something about the connection between her and Harry Miller. Imagine how this can further our investigation if I'm right."

"How will we justify our absence to Moretti? We've only been here twenty-five minutes. We are supposed to interview the tenants to try to find possible witnesses."

"Moretti will be happy if we make any progress. We have two murders and no potential evidence that could point us in the killer's direction."

He was right. So far, we had nothing.

"All right. Let's do it."

He pecked in a number on his phone, and somebody answered on the other end.

"Hey, Jensen, it's John ... yeah, it's been a while. Look, I've been digging into a recent crime, and something popped up that I think you might be able to help... Excellent. I'll be there at seven-thirty."

"We are lucky to have called now. Two minutes later he wouldn't have answered because he was going for a swim. He'll meet us in front of his building at seven-thirty."

"Where does he live?"

"Bal Harbour. Not far from where you live."

CHAPTER 4

The rush hour was coming to an end. My stomach started making strange noises, and I realized I had not eaten anything all day. And the day wasn't over yet.

"Who is this Jensen we are going to meet? "I asked John.

"He's my brother's private investigator agency partner. If I'm not mistaken, the victim worked for them."

"Why didn't you contact your brother?"

"He's out of town."

"Jensen is a Danish name. Is he Northern European?"

"He is a true New Yorker."

"Oh! I hope he has some answers for us."

"I hope so, too."

It was a good half hour before we arrived in Bal Harbour Village, a shining enclave at the northern tip of Miami Beach.

John slowed as he pulled into the parking lot of a condo building.

"We are too early," he said. "Let's grab a coffee somewhere."

"I drank too much coffee today. I prefer to walk on the beach to clear my thoughts."

"Okay, then. Here at seven-thirty."

I walked across the grass belt, feeling the sea breeze tickle my skin. It was the golden hour. A large sailboat slid regally across the water into a majestic sunset. Suddenly, just as the sun began to set, I was drawn to a swimmer gliding effortlessly through the water. When the outline of his strong shape loomed in the reddish light of the sunset, I had the impression of seeing the ghost of the God of Thunder, Thor, coming out of the water.

He was more than six feet tall, muscular, and absurdly good-looking in a rugged, masculine way. I stared at him for an endless moment, paralyzed with a strange, unfamiliar need, entirely captivated by his appearance. Finally, I became aware that he was getting closer. I tore my eyes away from him and returned to the parking lot. John was leaning against the car, sipping coffee.

"So, did you clear your thoughts?" he asked me.

"A little. It's so peaceful on the beach now, and the sunset is beautiful. It's like being in heaven."

"Miami is supposed to be a city of sun and endless fun."

"Is supposed to," I said. "But the countless forms of hideous death I have witnessed lately make me believe that hell is empty and all the devils are here."

"Speaking of the devil, here comes Jensen," John said.

"I turned around and saw the swimmer who had caught my eye a few minutes earlier. He was so attractive that I was dumbfounded. His eyes were a deep blue, like the colour of the crystal-clear water where magnificent sea creatures swim.

"Hey, mate," he said, shaking John's hand. "And who is this beautiful lady?" he asked, looking up at me.

"This is Detective Liv Olsen, my partner," said John, putting his hand on my shoulder.

"Hi. Jensen Hunt." He held my eyes briefly, shook my hand, and turned his attention to John.

"What can I do for you?"

"We are investigating a double murder. I'm not sure, but I think I saw one of the victims in your office a few weeks ago. I hope I'm right. Let me show you her picture."

He took out his phone and showed Jensen the picture. For a long moment, Jensen stared at the sight.

"Well?" asked John impatiently. "Do you know her?"

"Yeah. Her name is Briana Cooper. She worked for us. We gave her the cases we weren't interested in, like the follow-ups of unfaithful spouses."

John glanced at me, and I realized we were thinking the same thing: maybe Harry Miller was having an affair, and the killer was the vengeful husband.

"Are there any leads?" asked Jensen.

"None," answered John. "Liv thinks the same person killed both victims, and our blood spatter analyst agrees with her."

"Who is the other victim?"

"Harry Miller, the head of Sunshine Build Group, a construction company," John said while showing Jensen Harry Miller's photo.

"Jesus! It looks like an execution to me!" exclaimed Jensen. "Only a sick person can do something like that!"

"We agree on that," said John.

"So, you want to know if Briana had a file on Harry Miller or if she had a personal relationship with him," concluded Jensen.

"Exactly," said John.

"It has to wait until tomorrow morning; our secretary handles Briana's files. I will let you know."

"Thanks, Jensen," said John.

We shook hands with Jensen, and we got into the car. My heart was pounding. No man had ever struck me like Jensen Hunt, and I could not fathom why. I felt foolish and bravely attempted to calm down and gather my thoughts.

"This crime looks like good old-fashioned revenge," said John, bringing me down to earth. "Tomorrow, we will know more after we have the results of the labs, the autopsy, and possibly a connection between the victims."

"Hopefully, someone saw the killers when they dumped Briana Cooper's body."

"It will be pure luck."

"Which we need," I said in a hopeful voice. "Let's see if our team has progressed with the queries."

When we arrived at the crime scene, Maria Sanchez was questioning a short man. He looked intimidated by her tone and badge. She was pushing at him verbally, perhaps hoping he would give her a clue about the killers. Then she saw us and let him go. She snapped her head around and looked at us rather angrily.

"Where the hell have you been? Moretti has been looking for you everywhere!"

We told her about the information we'd gotten.

"At least you got something," she muttered. "What I got is nothing. Nobody saw anything, heard anything. Nothing."

Her eyes glazed and refocused on something on the other end of the parking lot. A news van was rolling in.

"Those assholes will be all over us in a minute," she snorted.

"Where are the others?" John asked her.

"Interviewing the tenants. I'll join Michael on the second floor, and you can start on the third floor."

"Let's do it," I said.

We knocked on the first door and took out our badges. A man in his forties opened the door.

"Police. We want to ask you a couple of questions," said John. "May we come in?"

The man reluctantly opened the door. I always hated interviewing people at home, especially when they were getting ready to relax after a long day at work. But this was all part of the bargain, all part of the determination to see justice done.

We knocked on several doors for the next few hours and asked the same questions. Unfortunately, no one had seen or heard anything. Around eleven-thirty, we decided that it was enough for the day.

"This case is more complicated than I thought," John said as we walked to the car.

"Some cases are like a puzzle, and you discover a skilled monster with each piece. But I'm sure we will catch him."

"Right now, we need a meal and a good night's sleep," John concluded.

I agreed with him. I was hungry and looking forward to going home, showering and sleeping. Little did I know, the game had just begun, and the sadistic psychopath would be one step ahead in a world of darkness, where the line between good and evil blur and the true nature of evil is bare.

CHAPTER 5

I woke up before dawn the next day, having slept fitfully. Even dozing, my mind had played and replayed the encounter with Jensen. An involuntary shiver ran down my spine. I was irritated, bewildered, and confused. I was falling for a man who probably didn't even remember I existed.

I quickly showered and turned on the TV while getting dressed to see the latest news. Every channel had the same information: *"The dead woman discovered yesterday is Briana Cooper, thirty-one years old, from Miami. The police are asking anyone with information to come forward and speak to them in confidence."*

I got to work a little later than usual, and the building was already buzzing with frantic activity. The press room was overflowing with people; cameras and microphones were everywhere, and there was no sign of Sergeant Moretti. Usually, he took every opportunity to see his picture published in the newspapers. He wasn't present this time because he had nothing to say to them.

I was just about to pour a cup of coffee when John

appeared and signalled me to hurry up: the briefing was supposed to start in two minutes.

"Jensen emailed me this morning, and guess what?" he asked.

"What?"

"Jeff Miller had hired Briana Cooper to keep his father under watch."

"Perhaps he knew his father was in danger. We need to talk to him."

"Until then, let's see if forensics have some answers for us."

As we entered the briefing room, we noticed that everyone else had already gathered, their attention focused on the unfolding situation. The laboratory analysis provided a significant revelation. The blood discovered at the crime scene, where Harry Miller tragically lost his life, was determined to belong to both him and Briana Cooper. This discovery shed light on the peculiar absence of blood at the location where Briana Cooper's body was found. Our hopes rested on the upcoming lab results, which we anticipated would offer more conclusive evidence. "It's becoming increasingly evident that the same perpetrator was behind both of these tragic deaths," John remarked.

"The frustrating part is that the forensics team hasn't uncovered any leads that could point us toward his identity," I said, voicing my disappointment.

"We might have to rely on the pending lab results for a breakthrough."

"We do have one lead, though," John speculated. "Jeff Miller had been keeping a close watch on his father, and there might be a connection between that surveillance and the crimes. So far, we're the only ones with a lead. Let's hope Moretti recognizes its significance and assigns us the case."

Fortunately, Moretti did grant us the case. We scored

a modest victory. Yet, the challenges ahead would be substantial, and we'd likely require assistance unravelling this intricate puzzle.

"Our first step should be paying a visit to Jeff Miller to understand why he hired Briana Cooper," I suggested.

John agreed, and we headed for the parking lot. The morning rush had subsided, and within minutes, John skillfully navigated us to the vicinity of the Sunshine Build Group building. As he made a series of swift turns, we descended the long, tree-lined driveway, ultimately reaching an open area adorned with brown and tan paving stones.

The structure before us left an indelible impression. Grey marble hallways were decorated with hanging plant baskets, creating a striking ambience.

A courteous smile graced the secretary's face as we approached.

"Good morning. How can I assist you today?" she asked.

"We are here to meet Mr. Jeff Miller," said John.

"Do you have an appointment?" she inquired. "Unfortunately, we do not," replied John.

We reached into our pockets, retrieved our badges, and displayed them for her. After a brief phone conversation, she gestured for us to follow her and guided us into what appeared to be a conference room.

"Mr. Miller will be with you shortly," she announced, leaving the room.

There were many photos on the walls showing Jeff Miller and his father with the mayor of Miami, political figures and famous people in show business, and images in which the Millers, surrounded by staff members, proudly showed the awards they received.

"There's no doubt that the Millers are well connected," I said, pulling out my phone and making a copy of every photo.

"What are you doing?" asked John.

"We must use every piece of information that can give us a lead."

At that precise moment, the door opened, and a man of average height walked toward us.

"Good morning, Detectives," he said in a deep voice. "Sorry to keep you waiting. I'm Jeff Miller. I assume your visit is related to my father's death?"

"Good morning, Mr. Miller. I'm Detective John Freeman, and this is my partner, Detective Liv Olsen. And you guessed right. Our visit is related to your father's death. Sincere condolences," said John.

"Thank you. Will this take long? I'm kind of in a hurry," said Jeff Miller.

"We have just a couple of questions, Mr. Miller," I said. "It will take only a few minutes."

"I hope I can answer your questions."

"We hope so too. We know that at the time of his death, you had your father under surveillance," I began. "We would like to know why."

"Surveillance? I don't know what you're talking about." Jeff Miller replied.

I couldn't help but glance at John. He seemed as surprised as I was by Miller's answer.

"Mr. Miller," I said. "We have evidence that you contacted a private investigator and put your father under surveillance. We want to know what the reason was," I insisted.

"And I repeat that you are wrong!" Jeff Miller replied. "I have never contacted a private investigator. I had no reason to. You have been misinformed."

He seemed sincere, so I decided to drop the subject.

"Did you notice anything strange about your father lately?"

"Like what?"

"Like anything. Had he been acting differently?"

"No. Nothing different."

"Mr. Miller, I have no choice but to ask you a very personal question. Do you know if your father was having an affair?"

"I was expecting this question, and I assure you that my father has never been unfaithful to my mother. He intended to retire soon to spend more time with her."

"What about your mother? Maybe she was the one having an affair?"

"Never!" he answered with a bit of irritation.

"Any idea who might have wanted to harm your father? Did you notice if anyone was angry with him?"

"There was always a competitor who was angry with my father. At the time of his death, we competed with another construction company for a ninety-million-dollar contract."

"Do you think they could commit such a violent act to win the contract?"

"No! They are not stupid. They knew that this competition would put them first on the list of suspects."

"Who was the competing company on this contract?"

"Skilled Builders Inc."

"Have you had any complaints from your employers lately? Is there anyone in particular who was unhappy with their income or working conditions? Somebody who was fired?"

"My father was a much-loved boss. He always found the time and met with the dissatisfied workers."

He glanced at his watch and stood up from his chair.

"Sorry, Detectives, but I must leave you. I hope you find the monster who killed my father."

He had tears in his eyes and looked like he was having a hard time coping with the pain of his father's death.

"Here are our business cards; contact us if you think of something that could help us in the investigation," said John.

"I will," he said as he left the conference room.

The information we depended on that might lead us to the killer led us to nothing. We were entirely in the dark unless the results we were expecting from the labs would provide us with some hints.

"We are back to square one," John sighed. "Did you believe him?"

"Unless he is the best actor I have ever seen, I think he was sincere. It's possible that someone else hired Briana Cooper, posing as Jeff Miller. We need Briana Cooper's file. It may contain information that can help us."

"You're right. I'll notify Jensen that you'll be stopping by tomorrow morning. The agency is on your way to work."

"Of course," I said, hoping that he did not decipher the emotion I felt at the thought of seeing Jensen again.

Once in the car, John called Philippe. He answered almost immediately.

"Philippe Balu."

"Philippe, this is John."

"Hey, buddy. What's up?"

"Are there any results from the labs?"

"Not yet. Our medical examiner is doing the autopsy right now. Let's hope he finds something."

"Thank you, Philippe."

John hung up and turned to me. "What now?"

"I think we need to go see Mrs. Miller," I said. "Who better to know if something was going on with her husband."

"You're right. Let's go."

CHAPTER 6

When John left the parking lot, I had already typed the Millers' address into the GPS. Naturally enough, the Millers lived in Gables Estates, one of South Florida's most sophisticated and prestigious communities along the beautiful waters of Biscayne Bay and the canals of the Intracoastal Waterway.

We were close to US-1 South when our cellphones started to chirp; a new case and another life lost. What surprised us was that the address sent by dispatch was the same as the one we were going to: The Millers.

"Damn!" snorted John, stepping on the gas pedal. "Someone decided to beat us to it. I imagine the victim must be another member of the Miller family."

"It sure looks like it."

"People hold grudges and seek revenge, but this one is outraged."

"Or sick. That's madness."

"It will take us thirty minutes to get there. Our team will get there before us."

He covered the distance to the Millers' house in twenty-five minutes. A modest crowd had gathered by the yellow barrier put up by the police.

While John was parking the car in front of the property entrance gates, a car slid to a halt beside us, and Moretti got out. The uniformed cops recognized him and moved aside as Moretti walked toward the house.

We got out and followed, the gravel crunching beneath our shoes.

"It's unbelievable! "exclaimed Tom Bishop when he saw us. "I have never seen anything so violent."

A few minutes later, I had to admit that he was right. The killer had turned the Millers' home into a slaughterhouse. The body of a man in his fifties lay in the entrance hall; his throat was slit with a single blow from a sharp knife, and his blood clotted on the walls. Ten feet away was the body of a woman who had suffered the same fate, her body looking like that of a broken doll. It was a full minute before I could breathe normally again.

Soon, I found myself standing in what seemed to be the living room, putting on plastic gloves, a bit disturbed by the violence to which the third victim had been subjected. I was informed the victim was Mrs. Miller, Harry Miller's wife. Her body was hanging from a rope attached to a crystal candelabra, and her lower abdomen had a significant cut.

The cuts on her body had been done with neatness and care. There was blood all over the walls and furniture. A lot of blood. It was almost like a replica of her husband's crime scene.

Every monster follows a series of rituals that make sense only to him and will never make sense to a normal human being. I looked around the room, and I saw John peering sternly at Miller's wife's body.

"Those motherfuckers are sicker than I thought," he said. "Judging by the footprints that he found, Philippe thinks they are the same ones who killed Briana Cooper and Harry Miller. Do you agree with him?"

"One hundred percent. Don't you?"

"I want to catch those assholes," he said instead of answering my question. "Have you got anything yet?"

"No. Do you know who found the bodies?"

"A friend of the victim, Mrs. Klein. You can find her in the kitchen."

I headed to the kitchen, telling myself that no punishment is too severe for somebody capable of committing crimes like these. A stout, elegantly dressed woman was sitting on a chair, crying.

"Mrs. Klein?"

"Yes. And who are you?"

"Detective Liv Olsen. I want to ask you some questions."

"Detective? Oh, dear! You should be in the fashion business rather than being a detective."
I was used to this reaction from people who didn't know me, so I ignored her remark.

"Was it you who discovered Mrs. Miller's body?" I asked her.

"Yes … I called her at least five times last night, but she didn't answer. So, I decided to visit her today. I should have checked on her earlier."

"Why didn't you? You didn't think it was strange when she didn't call you back?"

"There were times when she wanted to be left alone. To be honest, I was a bit relieved. She couldn't stop going on about her husband's death."

"Well, maybe it was the worst thing that had ever happened to her."

"I know, I know. It's just that there is a limit to what you can hear repeatedly."

"Did you notice any change in her behaviour lately?"

"No, I hadn't noticed any change in her behaviour. She was her usual self. She was quite happy because her husband had promised that he would soon retire and finally be able to spend more time together."

It confirmed what Jeff Miller had told us about his father's retirement.

"Mrs. Klein, do you know if Mr. Miller was having an affair?

"Oh, dear! No! Harry loved his wife!"

"What about Mrs. Miller?"

"Absolutely not!"

"Any idea who might have wanted to harm Mrs. or Mr. Miller?"

"Well … Harry was a ruthless businessman. He was getting most of the big contracts, which the competition did not like. My mother used to tell me that money is the devil's eye. Maybe his competitors had decided to eliminate him. I think they are the ones you should investigate."

"We will. Do you know the other two victims?"

"Yes. The man was the gardener, and the woman was the cook. They were distant relatives of Harry. Very good people."

"Did Mr. Miller have children from the previous marriage, or is Jeff the only child?"

"Jeff is the only child. Was he notified of his mother's death?"

"No, not yet."

"Oh, dear. Jeff will be devastated to have lost both his parents in such horrible circumstances."

Her face became ashen, and her eyes filled with tears. I put a hand on her shoulder.

"I'm sorry, Mrs. Klein. But I promise you, we will catch the killer. Here is my card. Call me if you think of anything to help us catch him faster."

We worked for the rest of the afternoon, using all our skills on flimsy evidence. Tom and Philippe did every test they could do on-site and found nothing significant.

Around five o'clock, everyone reconvened at headquarters, and we immediately got to business. I proposed the idea of placing Jeff Miller and his wife and children under surveillance, given that they were the sole surviving members of the family. Their safety could be at risk. Moretti concurred with my suggestion, assuring me he'd handle the task.

Maria Sanchez had meticulously gathered all the security camera recordings, and we commenced our examination, hoping to uncover any clues. While reviewing the Millers' house footage, we noticed that the thick foliage of the trees obstructed the view of the rear exit of the residence, creating a potential blind spot on the video feed for anyone to enter without detection.

By seven o'clock, I had stared at those tapes for an extended period, causing my eyes to ache, but our efforts had yet to yield any significant findings.

"Our killers are smart and are very good at what they do," I said. "And they don't leave prints."

"Mark my words, they're going to slip," said John. "And when they do, it's going to be the tiny details that allow us to crack this case wide open. We have to stay focused."

"Which means we have to wait for them to kill again and hope they make a mistake!"

"Look, Liv! I'm as frustrated as you are, but there's nothing more I can do or think about tonight. Let's go home and start again tomorrow morning with clear heads."

"Go home to your family, John. I'll stay a little longer. Nobody is waiting for me."

"It's none of my business, he said, but I have a hard time understanding how a stunning-looking woman like you has no one waiting for her. It's a waste."

With that, he waved goodbye and left the office.

I took a deep breath and continued to watch the footage. After only a few minutes, there was a sound at the door, and I looked up to see a cop I knew slightly.

"Detective Olsen, a man named Jensen Hunt wants to talk to you," he said.

My mouth almost popped open, and my heart started pounding frantically. I had always excelled at controlling my emotions, and thanks to my job, I learned to control them even more. I shook my head to gather my wits.

"Let him in," I told the cop.

And there was Jensen a few seconds later, looking relaxed and calm, totally unaffected by my presence. How unfair.

"Hello, Liv."

His voice was warm and husky, and there was a ghost of a smile on his lips.

"Hello, Jensen. What are you doing here?"

My question sounded more brittle than I intended, but instead of reacting with surprise at my rudeness, he smiled, and his eyes were alight with humour as he enjoyed my reaction.

"It's nice to see you too!" he said. "I was in the area and wanted to ask if you would have dinner with me?"

"How did you know I was still here?"

"I spoke with John. What about the dinner?"

"Sure, why not? I'm starving."

I resented how easily I fell under his spell but felt utterly destabilized by his presence.

"I know a small restaurant that has the best fish in town. You like fish?"

"I do like fish."

"Perfect. I took my motorcycle to avoid traffic jams. I hope you don't mind a motorcycle ride."

"I don't mind a motorcycle ride, but I was at a crime

scene all afternoon. I need a shower and a change of clothes. Pick me up in one hour."

"Right. Where do you live?"

I gave him my address.

"What? Really?" he exclaimed. "But this is a five-minute walk from where I live!"

"I know."

His frown became more quizzical.

"I'll pick you up in one hour."

I showered and got dressed. Then, for a wild second, I thought of calling and telling Jensen I had a headache and would rather stay home. But for some reason, I found that I could not. One hour later, I was ready to face him.

He drove along the coast road and eventually pulled into a seafood restaurant's parking lot. Inside, a waiter greeted him warmly.

"Detective Hunt! It's been a while since your last visit. Don't like our food anymore?"

"I do, Tony, but I've been swamped lately. Meet Detective Olsen," he said, turning toward me.

"Welcome to Il Pescatore, Detective Olsen," said Tony.

He smiled and led us to a table near the window. I started looking at the menu when Tony arrived with a dish of raw oysters on crushed ice.

"As usual," he said, addressing Jensen. "It is on the house."

"Thank you, Tony. I always order them when I come here," he said, gazing at me. "I hope you like oysters."

"I do."

I reached across, picked up an oyster, squirted some lemon juice, and let it slip down my throat. I licked my lips and realized Jensen was watching me intensely, his eyes hooded and heavy. I swallowed compulsively, trying to keep my face impassive as he spoke.

"What do you want for your main course?"

"As you are a regular customer, I'll let you decide."

"You won't be disappointed. What would you like to drink?

"Some white wine, please."

At that moment, my phone rang. I recognized my sister's number.

"Sorry, I have to answer this call," I said.

"No problem, go ahead."

"Hey, Sis."

"Liv, guess who I met in Paris! David! He's still crazy about you and…"

"Look, Sis," I said, interrupting her. "I can't talk to you right now. I'm at a restaurant having dinner. You're okay?"

"Never better. I'm having an amazing time."

"I can imagine. It's two-thirty in Paris, and you sound a little drunk. Be careful."

"Don't worry about me. I just wanted to know that you are okay. I miss you. Enjoy your dinner."

And she hung up.

My sister was undoubtedly in a nightclub and spoke loudly because of the overwhelming noise. I was sure that Jensen had heard the whole conversation even though he pretended not to pay attention.

"Sorry again," I said. "It was my sister."

"No worries. Is your sister on vacation in Paris?

"No, for work. My sister is a famous model."

He raised a brow.

"A model and a detective! Interesting! Why detective?"

"Life is about choices, and being a detective was mine. Why did you choose to be a private investigator?"

"It's a long story … let's say I like helping people."

Tony chose this moment to top up our glasses of water and whisk away our plates.

Moments later, he returned with our main course: Mahi-

Mahi with lemon and fine herbs served with vegetables and basmati rice.

The fish was delicious, and I closed my eyes to savour the taste better. When I opened them, I saw Jensen watching me, a slight smile on his lips.

"John tells me you're a New Yorker," I said, avoiding his gaze.

He grinned. "If what they say is true that someone born and raised in New York City or the New York City metropolitan area is a true New Yorker, it means that I am."

"Jensen means son of Jens and is of Scandinavian origin."

"Perhaps, but my ancestors come from Ireland."

"Would you like some dessert?" asked Tony as he approached the table to pick up our empty plates.

"No, thank you, Tony," I replied.

"We should go," I said to Jensen. "I had a hard day today, and it will be the same until we catch the killer. Thank you for the dinner."

"You're welcome."

"Did John notify you that I will stop by the agency tomorrow morning to pick up Briana's file?" I asked him.

"He did. That's why I brought the file home. I intend to study it before bed."

"Why?"

"Briana worked for us. I intend to do my investigation without jeopardizing yours."

"I hope something in the file will point us in a certain direction because we are completely in the dark."

"What do you say we go to my place and take a look together?"

Is he joking? Okay, I like him. I've never felt like this before. But that doesn't mean I have to have sex with him the first night.

"I'm tired," I said. "I'll pick it up tomorrow morning as

agreed."

A wide grin spread across his face, and he brushed back a wave of his sand-coloured hair.

"As you wish! But you wanted to know if there was a lead in Briana's file as much as I do. It's still early."

He seemed sincere, and I decided to trust him.

Maybe he's not even interested in me, and it's just my imagination. Besides, I'm impatient to see if I can find a lead in the file.

"You know what, you're right," I said. "I can't wait to see that file. Let's go."

CHAPTER 7

Traffic was heavy, and I understood why Jensen opted for the bike. Twenty-three minutes later, we were in the building where he lived. The elevator stopped at the top floor, and I followed Jensen into his apartment.

The size of the living room led me to conclude that it was a penthouse. It was large, bright, and sparsely furnished. The far wall was made of glass and led onto a terrace overlooking the sea.

"Not bad for a private detective!" I said.

"I'm not complaining. Something to drink? I have whisky, vodka, and bourbon."

"I'll have a whisky on the rocks."

We sat down and started reading Briana's report. Several pages detailed Harry Miller's whereabouts and a few pictures of him talking to different people. The file also confirmed that Jeff Miller was the one who had requested surveillance of his father. On the last page, Briana had written Jeff Miller's name and three exclamation marks, highlighting them with a yellow marker.

"Did you ask Jeff Miller why he kept his father under

surveillance?" asked Jensen.

"We did. That's what's surprising. He said he never asked a private investigator to watch his father."

"Hmm. Maybe he's right."

"What do you mean?"

He flipped through the report and pulled out a picture of Harry Miller surrounded by staff members.

"This is the picture Jeff Miller gave Briana to open the file. Why not a picture with only Harry Miller? A son should have several pictures of his father."

"Maybe it wasn't him who hired Briana. He seemed sincere when we talked to him."

"Which means she was hired by someone who pretended to be Jeff Miller," Jensen concluded.

"Exactly."

"That would explain why Briana had highlighted his name, followed by the exclamation marks. Maybe she was starting to have doubts. I suggest you put Jeff Miller under watch. He may be hiding something, but he could also be in danger. He is the only living member of the family."

"It's already done."

"I don't see anything else in this file to help us find the culprit. I'll check with our secretary in the morning to see if she remembers who hired Briana, and I'll let you and John know."

In other words, he wanted me to leave.

"You're right. Thanks again for dinner."

I got up to leave. Jensen closed the file and took his glass.

"Let's finish our drinks, and then I'll drive you home," he said.

"You don't have to. I can walk."

"Nonsense. Grab your drink, and let's go outside. It's a beautiful evening."

He approached a shelf with a sound system. Before long, soft music filled the room. Then he opened the patio door and stepped out onto the terrace. I followed him.

"Wow!" I exclaimed, looking around.

On the right side was an imposing white sofa, U-shaped, that could comfortably seat six people. Two deck chairs on the left were covered with pale blue cushions. There were tropical plants everywhere that spread a subtle fragrance in the air.

Slowly, the outside world invaded my senses.

The wind picked up a little, and a cool breeze blew from the sea. The pale crescent moon shone like a silvery claw in the night sky. The sound of waves mixed with the music, and all my self-control was floating away.

I watched Jensen from beneath my lashes. Blond locks framed the firm lines of his face with a strong jaw and prominent cheekbones. His skin was tanned, and his impressive build added a wildness to his beauty. He was so tantalizingly close and smelled so clean, fresh, heavenly. It was intoxicating. I was paralyzed with an unfamiliar need, entirely captivated by him.

I closed my eyes and took a deep breath, trying to recover what remained of my self-control. I had to get away from him.

"Would you like another drink?" he asked softly.

"No, thank you. I should go."

Jensen glanced at me and smiles. His look was so intense that I drowned in the depths of his blue eyes. I felt a strange intimacy between us, charging, filling the space with static.

He approached me and took my hands between his. They were large and strong. Their touch made me shiver, and I could feel the heat radiating from his palms and spreading throughout my body.

"You are so beautiful," he murmured.

He removed the ribbon that kept my hair, letting it cascade down my shoulders. One hand remained in my hair while the other travelled down my spine, hauling me against his body. My breath became shallow, rushed, and full of expectations.

"Do you have any idea how much I want you, Liv Olsen?"

"Don't," I heard myself say.

He pulled back suddenly, holding me at arm's length, carefully watching my reaction.

"Do you want me to stop? Or should I keep going?

He stared at me, his gaze hooded, his eyes darkening. Desire, hot and heavy, surged through my bloodstream.

My hands moved involuntarily to his shirt, stripping the fabric of his shoulders and arms. He gasped as I undid the last button and then he began a slow and sensual assault, caressing me, feeling his way through the dips of my skin. His body smelled divine, and I wanted to breathe the scent forever. I was all sensation, overwhelmed, in a place where desire had no limits. Jensen's gaze never left mine. He watched each reaction that his touch elicited from me.

It was three in the morning when he wrapped his arms around me and closed his eyes. He kissed my hair gently and inhaled deeply.

"You feel so good," he whispered.

I placed my head on his chest, closed my eyes, and fell asleep.

The morning light was pouring onto the terrace when I woke up. I stretched out and opened my eyes. Jensen was no longer beside me. I found my clothes scattered on the floor and quickly put them on. I crossed the living room, and I realized I could hear the shower running.

Do I stay? Do I go? I'd better leave before he finishes his shower to avoid an embarrassing situation. I took a last look around the living room and then headed straight for the door.

CHAPTER 8

One careful foot in front of the other, I slipped past the house and into the shadow of a hedge, and then I waited. Nothing moved. The street was quiet as if I was on the edge of a desert with miles of sand.

I was alone and unseen in the darkness, waiting for the moment that must come. A house like this should have been home to a family with children, not a filthy, bawdy house. People were losing touch with fundamental values.

I knew the well-regulated life of the two men I was about to kill, down to the slightest detail. The hunting would be good.

I heard a car's engine and, moments later, a key sliding into the lock. I held my breath, tensing my muscles, ready to burst into the house. The alarm system emitted its usual beep. I set off at a run and was at the door briefly.

"Not a sound," I said in a cold voice.

Recognition trickled onto their faces, and for a second, everything seemed suspended, as though time were folding in on itself. Their eyes went wider with terror when they saw the scalpel and the duct tape, and they understood this was just for them.

I watched them for a moment, letting the fear grow and the joy fill my emptiness. Then I leaped forward and drove the knife into the house owner's rib cage with a quick, brutal motion. He fell to his knees, and his breath came slower, but he was still alive.

I saw the boldness in the other one's eyes as he said sharply, "You are in so much fucking trouble! I'm going to have your ass in jail for this, you piece of shit!"

He was about to grab me when I drove the blade upward, causing irreversible damage to his sternum. I felt the warmth of blood touch my body and a swell of savage joy rising from a particular place inside.

But I still felt the need to be fulfilled. I needed to continue until I satisfied my innermost self's deep longings. The ritual had only just begun.

CHAPTER 9

I stretched out in the comfort of my bed, my thoughts wandering briefly to Jensen and the intensity of those wild, unique, irresponsible moments. I closed my eyes as my body hummed at the recollection, and my muscles contracted deep in my belly. How had he gotten under my skin so quickly?

I didn't want to think about it now. Maybe for him, I was just one of many "one-night stands." He was probably relieved I was already gone when he got out of the shower.

I shook my head to clear my thoughts. Either way, anything that started that hot was bound to burn out fast. I'd better save my time and the heartbreak.

I showered quickly and got dressed. As I drove to work through the usual rush-hour traffic, life slipped back into its ordinary routine.

At headquarters, the conference room was full of people. All of the significant dailies had sent reporters. I found John observing Sergeant Moretti, who was using a variety of phrases to convey the same message: he could not provide details because doing so might compromise certain aspects of the investigation. When the press conference ended, Moretti headed in our direction.

"Any development?" he asked.

"Nothing so far," said John.

"Did you see that?" Moretti exclaimed. "I'm under much pressure from the media, the public, and victims' families. I'm trying to buy you time, but the FBI is already breathing down my neck. If you still have nothing by Friday, you can kiss the case goodbye."

He turned around and walked into his office. He punched a metal file cabinet in a fury, which shuddered under the blow.

"He's crazy," said John. "Today is Thursday. And we still need the lab results! Cops need to be encouraged by their senior officer, not kicked in the ass."

"Don't worry about Moretti," I reassured him. "He's under a lot of pressure. This is a major investigation for him, and he wants to prove that he and his team can solve the case. An FBI intervention would only embarrass him. Let's not waste time on that."

He followed me to my desk, and I briefed him on the contents of Briana Cooper's file and the conclusions I drew from it.

"It might be possible that Jeff Miller is hiding something from us, and the only way to find out what is by confronting him with the evidence we have against him," I explained. "But we should not rule out the possibility that he was telling the truth and never contacted Briana Cooper."

"You're right. But we have nothing else to go on. Did you seen Jensen this morning at the agency? Do you know if he looked at the file?"

How was I to answer his questions? He thought I had stopped at the agency on my way to work to pick up the file, as agreed, and that I had studied it quickly. I decided it was better not to say anything for the moment. Sooner or later,

Jensen would tell him what happened between us.

"He intends to do his investigation," I said.

"I am not surprised. Did you ask his opinion?"

"I did, and I was astonished to see that we were pretty much in agreement in our conclusions."

"Why were you so surprised?"

"Let's say I didn't expect him to have the same logic as I do, even if he has accumulated experience since working as a private investigator. "

John burst out laughing.

"Jensen and my brother," he said, "are not just any private investigators. They have worked for the CIA for many years. My brother has been a great agent but doesn't compare to Jensen. He has rare mental agility and an unflinching nature in harrowing situations. Anecdotally, only some successful agents run in the high-120 IQ range. He is one of those. I won't be surprised if he finds the killer before we do."

"Then how come they end up being private investigators?" I asked, wondering why Jensen didn't mention that he had worked for the CIA.

"It's not my place to talk about that," said John.

"Fair enough. Let's see if the labs have sent anything."

"I don't think they did, but let's check it out anyway."

We found Philippe kneeling, looking for something in a cardboard box under his desk.

"Hey, Philippe," I said. "Did you find anything?"

"Except for the two different footprints, nothing," he answered. "I believe the smallest one belongs to a woman. So, I'm sure now that we are talking about two killers."

"Did you find a match in the database?"

"I couldn't find any match in the database. I'm sorry."

"What about the blood we found at the crime scene?" asked John.

"According to Tom, the blood belonged only to the

victims. We are up against very clever killers."

"Let's go see Gary," said John. "We may have more luck with the results from the autopsy."

We got into the car and headed toward the coroner's building. We found Gary Wilson, the medical examiner, leaning over Briana Cooper's body. I looked at the cuts, and I felt a cold shiver crawling across the back of my neck.

"Good to see you guys," Gary said. "But you're too early. I did not finish my examination."

"Quick question, Gary," I said. "Do you think it was the same person who killed them both?"

"And that he used the same weapon?" added John.

"That's two questions," Gary said. "Both victims had been killed with the same weapon. That answers your second question. But I don't think the same person killed them both."

"Considering the footprints he has found, Philippe believes there are two killers," I said.

"And he's right."

"Are you sure about that?" I insisted.

"The possibility of error is very low, practically zero," Gary answered.

His answers hung in the air.

"Can you give us more details?" I asked.

"Sure. There are small, insignificant details that can go unnoticed if you don't study them for hours, as I do. The wounds on Harry Miller's body were inflicted before his death. There are just a few patches of visible skin unmarked by trauma. To inflict such wounds and not kill the person, you need to have an extensive knowledge of human anatomy, like a doctor or an ER nurse. The wounds on Briana Cooper's body are rougher, as if they were hurried. Take a look."

He showed us the minor differences, and I had to agree he was right.

"What about the weapon?" asked John.

"I think it's a surgical knife, a scalpel."

"Can you figure out what kind of surgical knife was used in these crimes?" asked John.

"I can, but it will take a little time. Scalpel blades come in different sizes, identified by a blade number, each serving a different purpose."

"Can you find out which Miami medical facility uses this specific surgical blade?"

"Medical facilities use the best quality surgical blades because they play an important role in a surgical team's success. So, don't be surprised if several medical facilities use the same ones. Imagine also the number of people with access to those surgical blades."

"What else can you tell us?"

"Harry Miller died sometime between eleven and midnight after being tortured for hours. Briana Cooper was killed between four and five o'clock in the afternoon. There are no signs of struggle, which means the victims knew the killer or he overpowered them, so they didn't have a chance to fight back. I also think the two killers have committed many crimes together."

"What makes you believe that?" I asked.

"There is a similarity in their actions, which leads me to believe they've done it before, following the same ritual. You are looking for two cold-blooded killers who planned the murders with care. For some people, violence is part of their everyday life."

Like we don't know, I wanted to say. Violence is part of everyone's life. We're all constantly exposed to it. Genocide, bombings, and wars are routinely included in the continuous flow of barbarism coming from our TV screens.

"Is there something else?" I insisted.

"That's all for now. Let me continue my examination, and I will send you my report."

"Thank you, Gary," we said, heading out the door.

CHAPTER 10

Outside, the heat was overwhelming, and the car's air conditioning could barely cope. Our next stop was Sunshine Build Group to see Jeff Miller.

"Well… at least Gary got us a few promising leads," I said. "We know that the killer, or the killers, have some medical knowledge and that the murder weapon used was a scalpel."

"According to him, this is not their first crime," said John. "We have to check in the database if similar crimes have occurred."

"Moretti assured me there has never been a similar case in Miami. We must search the state database. And let's hope Jeff Miller will be more cooperative this time."

We drove south, moving smoothly through traffic, and twenty-seven minutes later, we found ourselves in the lobby of Sunshine Build Group. The secretary recognized us right away.

"Good morning, Detectives. What can I do for you?"

"We would like to see Mr. Jeff Miller," said John.

"Mr. Miller is not in today."

"Do you have any idea where he might be?"

"I guess at home. With everything that's happened, he may need to grieve."

"We need the address."

She wrote the address on a piece of paper and gave it to us. I wasn't surprised that Jeff Miller's home address was in Gables Estates, near his parents' house. It wasn't money they lacked. Driving around town, there were signs with the name Sunshine Build Group at nearly every construction site.

We found the house quickly. There was a surveillance car near the wrought-iron gate blocking off the driveway, meaning Moretti kept his word. The gate opened after we identified ourselves on the video intercom.

John parked the car in front of the house and paused after turning off the engine.

"Wow! Jeff Miller's garage is larger than my house!" he said. "But with their iron gates and the most sophisticated alarm systems, they are no more protected than we are."

As I glanced toward the garage, a pretty woman in her thirties opened the house door. She walked toward us slowly as we stepped out of the car.

"Hello, Detectives. I'm Debby Miller," she said, stumbling to a halt and staring at us.

She had a pale face, large eyes, and plenty of makeup. She looked tired and a little ill at ease.

"Hello, Mrs. Miller. I'm Detective Liv Olsen, and this is my partner, Detective John Freeman."

"Are you the detectives handling the case of my parents-in-law?"

"Yes, that's us," I said.

"Can I see your IDs?"

We reached in our pockets for our badges while Mrs. Miller paused cautiously, no doubt worried we might pull out a gun.

"Well," she said, looking from the badges to our faces

and quickly away again. "All right. Would you like to come in?"

"We came to talk to Mr. Miller," I said. "Is he home?"

"I would like to talk to Mr. Miller, too, but I haven't seen him since yesterday."

There was a bitterness in her voice.

"Do you know where he is?" I asked.

"With his … friend."

"Who is this friend?"

"Uh-huh, well…" she shrugged, seeming uncomfortable.

"Mrs. Miller," I said. "I need you to answer my question."

She bit her lip, and her eyes momentarily darted from side to side. Then she shivered and shook her head.

"Oh, what the hell," she finally said. "You'll know it anyway very soon. Now that his parents aren't around to stop him, he'll go public with it."

"What did you mean by that?"

She hesitated again as if fighting an inner battle, but finally, she decided to speak.

"Jeff has a boyfriend. We live in the same house only to keep up appearances and for the sake of our children."

"Do you have an address for your husband's boyfriend?

"I do."

She gave us an address in Coconut Grove.

"Have you been in contact with your husband since yesterday?" I asked.

"I called him this morning, but he didn't answer."

"Does he have a habit of not answering your calls?"

"No. Jeff usually answers my calls or calls me back to ensure everything is okay with the children."

"Did you get the impression that he was more preoccupied than usual lately? More anxious? Different?"

"My husband is deeply involved in his work. He is highly skilled in managing stress. I rarely see him anxious despite the heavy responsibilities he has to deal with every day. I didn't notice any change in his behaviour during the last few weeks. Except, of course, that he's sad about his parents' deaths."

"Do you have any idea who might have wanted to kill your parents-in-law?" asked John.

"I have no idea. The relationship between me and my in-laws could have been better. They considered me a failure because their son preferred men."

"Thank you for your time, Mrs. Miller."

"Any developments in my in-laws' case?"

"Not yet. But we're doing our best. We'll find the killer sooner or later."

As we rose to leave, an idea came to mind.

"One last thing, Mrs. Miller. What kind of car does your husband drive?"

"A Lincoln … black."

"Thank you again, Mrs. Miller."

She nodded. Returning to the car, I thought that Miller's life wasn't exactly the paradise that outsiders perceived it to be.

CHAPTER 11

We stopped quickly to buy coffee and bagels. It was a good half hour before we arrived at Jeff Miller's boyfriend's house, and we saw his car parked in the driveway. We strolled down the sidewalk toward the house and pressed the doorbell. No answer.

"Maybe the doorbell doesn't work," John said as he knocked and stood, glancing up at the dark clouds of the approaching storm.

There was no answer. I started to have a bad feeling.

"All right. Let's have a look," I said.

I pressed the door handle, and the door opened effortlessly. We notified anyone inside of our presence in a loud voice, but there was no response. We took out our weapons and advanced into the house.

Inside was dark; the curtains and blinds were all pulled closed. A doorway opposite the front door showed a small patch of light, and we headed that way. John pushed open the door, and I heard him whispering.

"Oh, God…"

But God wasn't anywhere around that day. He had given up his place to the Devil. I felt a weird sense of déja vu, the images of the last crimes parading through my head. Two men were hanging from the ceiling, their legs wrapped with tape, their faces set in tight masks of agony. One of them was Jeff Miller. Their genitals had been removed with neatness that would have made a surgeon jealous, although it seemed likely that no surgeons would be able to justify this kind of work. There was blood everywhere.

"Have you got any guesses about this?" asked John.

"Definitely not a fight with the boyfriend," I said. "Judging by the stab wounds, it is undoubtedly the same ones who killed his parents and Briana Cooper."

"It takes some careful planning to execute all these murders in such a short time," said John.

"The killers know that every cop in Miami will be working with extra diligence to catch them to become the city's heroes. They are being more than careful. Let's hope they made a mistake this time," I said.

While John returned to the car and notified dispatch by radio, I carefully examined the two bodies and looked through the rest of the house, desperately searching for some clues. I didn't find anything. I looked again, hoping I might have overlooked something the first time. Nothing. How was it possible to kill these vigorous young men and leave no evidence? It told me that the victims knew the killer and had no idea what he was up to.

I felt like I was fighting a shadow in a dark room. In the near distance, a siren wailed and was joined by another. Help was on the way. Within the next hour, the room became crowded with people. Sergeant Moretti arrived with Officer Maria Sanchez in tow. His face was set in a rigid, stony mask, meaning he was ruled by discipline and duty.

Despite the violence of the crime, the team went

about the business of collecting evidence. Photographs and measurements were taken, Luminol was sprayed, the area was dusted for prints, and the floor was analyzed for footprints. Everybody was working with relentless precision, recognizing the signature of the same killers who recently plunged the city into terror.

"Detective Olsen, what can you tell me?" asked Moretti.

"Double homicide. No weapons I could find, no forced entry."

"Do we know who the victims are?"

"One of the victims is Jeff Miller, Harry Miller's son."

"What the hell was he doing here? I put his house on surveillance, thinking he'd share the pain of losing his parents with his family!"

I filled him in on the information Jeff Miller's wife had given us.

"The second victim is his boyfriend," I added.

"Hmm…" muttered Moretti, looking at the mutilated bodies. "Officer Sanchez," he said to Maria, "why don't you go ahead and walk off the perimeter, canvass the area, see if anybody's heard or seen anything."

Then he turned toward me.

"I'll be giving a formal statement to the press soon. Do you know what their first question will be?"

"If we have any suspects?"

"That's right. And the problem is, we don't have any. If the case is too complicated for you, I will pass it to somebody else. I need to catch these psycho motherfuckers. You got it?"

He tended to lash out at someone when things didn't go his way; this time, it was me.

"Got it, Sergeant," I said.

I was gratified to see John step in and say," We're doing what we can, Sergeant. But you have to admit that these killers move so quickly from one victim to the next, leaving no evidence, that we haven't had the chance to find out who they are."

"Then you'll have to find a way to move faster than them; lives are at stake here," said Moretti.

John and I nodded without commenting and walked over to where Philippe was screening the floor for evidence.

"Did you find anything?" I asked him with little hope. He held up a plastic evidence bag. Inside was a half-used tape.

"What does that mean?"

"I have a fingerprint."

"Really?" I said.

"Really."

"Run the print," I said impatiently. "I want a name."

"It's a partial print, Liv. It could take a few days."

"We don't have a few days. We need the results as quickly as possible."

"This guy is moving fast," said Philippe. "Do you think he'll kill again?"

"I don't know, Philippe. Hopefully, he was just interested in the Millers."

"You know, these sadistic psychopaths are like wild animals; they stop killing when their hunger is satisfied."

"Yeah, Philippe. Until they get hungry again. Run the print."

"Will do."

I stepped outside, the cameras started flashing, and the reporters swung in my direction.

"Detective, tell us what's going on. Detective…"

"I can't comment," I told them. "I'm sorry. There will be a formal statement."

I was moving toward one of the yellow crime scene tapes when a big man, well-muscled and dressed in a lovely suit, approached me. There was something familiar about him.

"Uh, hello, Detective," he said.

"How can I help you?" I asked, wondering where I had seen him before.

"Can you tell me if Jeff Miller is one of the victims?"

"What makes you think that Jeff Miller is one of the victims?" I replied. "And who are you?"

"I'm sorry. My name is Robert Wilson. I'm the attorney of Sunshine Build Group. I came to get a signature from Jeff."

That's when I realized why his face looked familiar: I had seen him in the photos hanging in the company's conference room.

"How did you know he would be here? Why didn't you go to his house?"

"Well, he told me yesterday that I'd find him here if needed. Since he didn't answer my call, I took the chance to come, hoping to find him. I see that his car is in the driveway."

"I'm afraid I can't give you any details, Mr. Wilson. As an attorney, you understand that."

"Of course."

I'm not paranoid, but I sensed he was scrutinizing me, and there was an icy look on his face for a moment.

"Do you mind giving me your business card? I intend to ask you some questions about the Miller family."

He smiled briefly and pulled a business card from his briefcase.

"Of course. Anything I can do to help."

"Thank you, Mr. Wilson."

I observed him navigating the bustling crowd with great care. I contemplated how I had successfully solved every homicide case I'd taken on until now. This one may prove to be the exception. The murderer was swift, transitioning from one victim to the next, leaving little opportunity to pursue any leads.

The wailing police sirens abruptly snapped me back to

reality, and my cellphone began to ring. Sensing a presence behind me, I swiftly turned around, only to find John standing there.

"Here you are," he said. "There was a shooting in the neighbourhood. Moretti is already there, waiting for us. He thinks there is a connection with our case."

"I heard the sirens. Let's see if Moretti is right."

CHAPTER 12

It was a quick drive to the crime scene. Three squad cars were parked in the house's circular driveway; their doors hung open, and the flashers were still on. While we showed our IDs to the officer in charge, more cars filled with detectives pulled up in front of the house. A man in his forties was lying on the carpet inside the house. A wound near his heart had left a large pool of blood on the floor. The overturned furniture suggested a violent argument between the victim and someone else.

"What happened?" John asked one of the police officers.

"A marital dispute. It is not the first time that's happened. Police reports prove that the victim was a very violent man. His wife is the only person who can tell us exactly what happened."

"Is she here?"

"She is in the bedroom and does not want to come out. Detective Michael Bennett tried to convince the woman to open the door unsuccessfully. She said that if we opened the door, she would kill herself. She has a gun."

We approached the bedroom.

"Michael," I said. "Let me try. Perhaps a woman's voice can reassure her."

"Go ahead. I don't think she's going to buy it."

"Do you know her name?"

"Victoria Green."

I walked over to the door.

"Mrs. Green, I'm Detective Liv Olsen. I'm going to open the door. All right?"

I slowly opened the door. A woman was sitting on the floor, and as I entered, she pointed the gun at her head. Her face was swollen, and there were bruises on her arms.

"Hold it, Mrs. Green. Please. Look, I'm going to close the door. I'm going to sit right here, okay? But I want you to put the gun down. I need to confirm a couple of things with you. For instance, did your husband beat you often?"

Slowly, she moved the weapon away from her head and started talking.

"After each beating, he promised me that he would stop, that it would never happen again. He beat me so badly this time that I decided it would be the last time."

"I think you did what you had to do, Mrs. Green. Is it all right if I come a little closer?"

She seemed to agree, so I moved closer.

"Thank you, Mrs. Green. Now, all we have to do is photograph your bruises to show the reason that led you to such drastic action. But no one will ever know the truth if you pull the trigger. Can I have the gun?"

She pondered for a moment, but finally, she gave it to me. I helped her to get up, and we stepped outside the room.

"Mrs. Green, this is Detective Bennett," I said, pointing to Michael. "He will recommend the best lawyers who specialize in battered women's defences. Isn't that right, Detective Bennett?"

"Of course," Michael answered as he handcuffed her.

"Good job, Detective Olsen," said John, tapping me on the shoulder.

"Thanks."

"Well, if you two are done here," said Moretti, suddenly materializing at our side, "we still got a cold-blooded killer on the loose. I'm going to notify Mrs. Miller of her husband's death. I'll see you later at headquarters."

John glared at me. His expression meant: "he's still kicking our ass."

We rolled across town, mostly keeping our thoughts to ourselves. We stopped for a bite and more coffee, and by four o'clock, we got to headquarters. One of the conference rooms had been set aside for for the Miller's family's case, and it was already buzzing with activity when we strolled in. Moretti was sitting at a large table that was heaped with lab reports, maps, and coffee cups. He looked up at John and me and beckoned us to join him.

"All right," he said in a loud voice. "I need all your attention for a minute. So far, we have no leads. We are damned lucky we don't have the FBI in here yet. But it won't last long."

I wanted to mention that the FBI gets involved in a criminal case only if a federal offence was committed, but I think he knew that and just wanted to put pressure on us.

"As you know," he continued, "I assigned the case to Detectives Olsen and Freeman. But they need all the help they can get. I'll let them tell you what they have to date."

A heavy silence fell over the investigation team.

"As many of you are aware," John began, "we thought that the recent murders were motivated by revenge against the Miller family. The killer moved so quickly from one victim to the next, leaving us no time to follow any leads. Our medical examiner is convinced that we are looking for two cold-blooded killers who planned the murders with care.

The similarity in their actions leads him to believe they've done it before and that it is the work of serial killers. I don't have much experience in serial killer cases, so I will leave that to Detective Olsen. I'm sure she has dealt with similar cases while working with the FBI."

He beckoned me to begin. I took a sip of coffee and cleared my throat.

"I came to the same conclusion as the medical examiner," I said. "I think two serial killers committed the crime. I shared my opinion with Sergeant Moretti at the crime scene, and he assured me there had never been a similar case in Miami. But they could have killed elsewhere."

"I think it is too early to talk about serial killings," intervened Moretti. "Serial killers usually choose their victims at random. In this case, the killer was after specific targets: members of the Miller family. The whole thing was too organized, too structured to be the work of a serial killer. I don't think that's what's going on."

Moretti did not like being contradicted, but I supported my theory.

"Serial killings appear to be entirely random at first; each victim may have something in common that only the killer quickly recognizes," I said. "Often, there is no rational explanation for why a person chooses a particular victim. Some have a scenario playing out in their mind, and it's all about situations that suit their fantasy rather than a specific victim type. The feelings of revenge and hatred are often driving forces behind their crimes. In these situations, the rate of violence is higher than in the other crimes he has committed. I believe these were the two reasons in the Miller family's case."

"What makes you think this is a serial killer? Maybe it was just revenge," insisted Moretti.

"The knife cuts were so thorough, beyond normal,

comfortable, and I found it disturbing. It required remarkable strength and, most frightening, incredible control during the whole process. This seemed like a pattern, and I'm firmly convinced it was not a single episode where somebody had decided to take revenge."

"You can't be sure of that," Moretti insisted again.

"I'm almost sure. People do not become serial killers overnight. It develops over a very long time. Think of it as an addiction. Like the person with a heroin addiction, he's always seeking that elusive first high. He takes his fantasies and turns them into reality. And he's doomed to fail. That's why the period between crimes is getting shorter, and the offence becomes more elaborate. And he will carry on feeding that killing habit."

"Are the victims chosen?" asked Maria.

"Every serial killer has a victim type. They are not victims of chance. They are victims of choice. They don't know him, but he knows them. Staking his victims is part of his ritual. It makes him feel superior to the rest of us mere mortals. It's about power, control, and the thrill. In his mind, he feels he has the right to decide who lives and who dies."

"Then let's get to work, said Moretti. I want every investigation team member to concentrate on finding a lead."

"The fact that there are several of us and just two of them doesn't mean we have the advantage," I said. Don't let appearances fool you. They frequently appear to be charming, intelligent, and charismatic. They move around in their darkness, and we operate under the glare of media lights."

"Okay, everyone, we got a lot to cover, so let's get started, said Moretti. We won't stop until we catch those sadistic psychopaths. Let's ensure we don't let anything slip through the cracks."

"Will do, Sergeant," John said, motioning for me to follow him.

CHAPTER 13

I need more coffee. How about you?" John asked me.
"I was hoping you'd ask."
While the coffee brewed, we headed to the lab to see if Philippe had a match for the fingerprint he found at the crime scene. We found him putting something in a small plastic bag using tweezers. He looked back over his shoulder and saw us.

"Detectives?"

"Any progress?" I asked.

"No match on the fingerprint. There is nothing to go on. The only lead I can think of, from how those sadistic psychopaths committed the crimes, is that it was a ritual."

"Are you thinking of a cult?"

"Yes. There are all kinds of reasons that can drive someone to commit a murder: money, jealousy, vengeance. But not in the way the Miller family members were killed; I think it is a sect that performs ritual sacrifices. I also believe its devotees are very clever. They may be upstanding members of society, entirely beyond suspicion in the light of the day."

"Well, I don't know if we are dealing with a cult, but it looks like the perfect crime," said John.

"There is no such thing as a perfect crime," I said. "Sooner or later, we will find out who did this. Let's see what Tom has to say."

We went across the hall to Tom's little cubicle off the forensics lab.

"The pattern of the blood indicates several important things," explained Tom. "There were certainly two killers. One is over six feet tall, while the second is only five feet, four inches."

"How on earth did they get away with this without leaving any evidence?" exclaimed John.

Tom nodded vigorously. "I know, right?" he said.

"What else can you tell us?" I asked Tom.

"There's no evidence of defensive wounds on the victim's body. Maybe he was too fearful and thought cooperation would make things better. Or, as Gary concluded, the killers overpowered him, so he didn't have a chance to fight back. They had things under their control, making me think this was not their first crime. They are both right-handed. But so are a few million people in Miami. I flipped the medical examiner report, and the condition of the internal organs on Harry Miller's body confirmed what the exterior tissue indicated: the killer had kept the victim alive as long as possible while torturing him with a vicious force."

"We've received the medical examiner report?" John asked.

"Yes. A few minutes ago. But only Harry Miller's."

"That means the report came in while we were with Philippe," said John.

Indeed, the medical examiner's report was waiting on my desk. I read the several pages detailing the massive trauma to which Harry Miller had been exposed, but there was nothing on the report that I didn't already know.

I had barely finished reading it when my desk telephone rang. I picked up the receiver.

"Olsen."

It was Lee Wang, the crime analyst.

"Did you read the medical examiner report?" he asked.

"Just finished it," I said.

"Are you with John? I have something for you."

"We'll be right there."

There was a lot of noise as John and I walked through the corridors. As usual, it was a busy day at the Miami Police Department. Neighbours in conflict almost killed each other, criminals, and drug dealers. Nothing was missing. Detective Maria Sanchez was handcuffing a very tall man with a shaved head, unimpressed by his adjectives.

"Yeah, baby, plug me in," he was saying.

Maria opened her mouth and then closed it again. Her eyebrows crashed together, and her lips got very thin.

"Don't listen to what he says, Maria," says John. "He's just playing with you."

"But I'm not," replied Maria. "He'll be an old man before he exits prison."

At that moment, two officers approached and grabbed the man.

"Keep up the good work, Maria," said John while we were walking away, "and soon you'll become Detective."

We found Lee Wang staring at his computer. He didn't seem to notice our presence.

"I'll see you're busy," I said, breaking him out of his frozen state.

"Ah! Excuse me, Detectives, I didn't hear you coming in. I have good news. As you asked, I combed the entire Florida state database. At first, I didn't find anything, but you know how I am. I don't give up easily, so..."

"Lee, we know you are one of the best crime analysts," said John impatiently. "Cut to the chase, and tell us what you found."

"All right. I discovered criminal cases similar to the Miller family's when digging deeper into the database. I believe there is a connection."

"In Miami?"

"No, in Jacksonville. Twenty years ago."

"Are you sure?" I asked. "It's been a long time. There are similarities in some crimes without being connected."

"Error is always possible. But this was stretching past the breaking point. Let me show you."

He turned to his computer and clicked on one of the folders on the desktop. The screen swirled and displayed the images of several corpses who had something in common: they were all hanging, their genitals had been removed, and there were what appeared to be stab wounds on the skin. There was also a lot of blood.

Whoever had done this had clearly enjoyed what he was doing. But compare it to the present crimes, his or their technique was clumsy, inefficient, even brutal, like they were exploring, seeking something they had not entirely found. Of course, it could have been a simple coincidence, but the resemblance was so apparent that it would be stupid not to consider Lee's conclusion.

"You may be right," I said.

"And get this," said Lee, with a satisfied smile. "The murder weapon used was a scalpel."

"Did they catch the killer?" asked John.

"They didn't. It's a cold case. The file should be in the Jacksonville Police Department archives."

"It can be the same killer, or it can be a copycat," I said. "Either way, it's something to be checked out."

"Just remember that forensic science was not as advanced

back then as it is today," said Lee. "There are many files in the police archives, cases that could have been solved with today's advanced methods."

"Perhaps we can convince Moretti to help us get this old file," I suggested.

"I don't think so," said John. "Especially since there hasn't been a similar case in twenty years."

"We don't know that," I said. "Lee only checked in the Florida state database."

"Liv is right," said Lee. "Let me check further. It should take some time; professional cooperation is a great idea, but most cops already have an overwhelming caseload. I'll let you know if I find something similar in another state."

"Let's start convincing Moretti to let us go to Jacksonville and see that old file," I suggested. "If we're lucky, we can talk to the detective who handled the case."

"Let's do it before he leaves," said John. "It's already seven o'clock."

We found Moretti pacing the room, examining the day's newspaper.

"I suppose you've seen the front pages today," he said as soon as we entered his office.

"Yes, we have," John answered.

"The eyes of the public are upon us. The media has their stopwatches out, timing how long it takes us to find the culprits. They're waiting for us to slip up so that they can crucify us. Tell me that we have a lead. Don't tell me we've hit the wall," he said, looking at us expectantly.

John looked at me with a very uncomfortable expression.

"I think we have a lead," I replied. "Nothing certain yet, but we think we know where to look now."

Moretti's eyes lit up.

"Interesting. Let's hear it."

He listened to us without interrupting. Then, there was a

brief silence during which he studied the file Lee had prepared on the crimes committed twenty years ago in Jacksonville.

"Well, I think it's a start," he said. "The similarities are there."

"So, is that a yes?" asked John.

"Yeah. It's a yes. But our budget is limited, only one of you can go. Detective Olsen, I'll give you the lead, so you'll go to Jacksonville. Take the first flight tomorrow morning, and I'll ensure they provide you with access to the file. You, Detective Freeman, may begin interviewing those who can give us information about the Miller family."

I was surprised that he gave the lead to me rather than John, especially since he showed little confidence in my abilities.

John stared at Moretti briefly, and I expected him to oppose the decision. Instead, he headed for the door fast enough that I had to hurry, and I only caught up once he was at the entrance to the parking lot.

"Look, John. He didn't mean anything by giving me the lead," I said.

"That's horseshit, and you know it. But it has nothing to do with you. That's between Moretti and me."

"I think you're overreacting."

"Maybe. Anyway, I'm going home. It would be best if you went home too. Tomorrow you have a long day."

I watched him go, turned, and walked back to my office. I sat in my chair and got down to work. Or, to be perfectly accurate, I got down to organizing what I knew, and one hour later, I felt like I was at something of a dead end. I was done for the day.

As the elevator doors slid shut, I closed my eyes, and my mind drifted to the moments spent with Jensen. I had been waiting to hear from him all day. I shook my head in irritation and walked to the parking lot. I didn't want to examine my feelings for him. I was frightened of what I'd uncover. Luckily, my phone rang at that moment, and I hurried to answer, relieved to change my thoughts.

"Olsen."

"Hello, Liv."

Jensen's voice sent little shivers down my spine.

"Hello, Jensen."

"You left this morning without a word."

"Isn't that what men want the morning after? To save themselves the embarrassment of asking the woman to leave?"

"Women usually don't leave unless I ask them to. And I didn't wanted you to leave."

"Well … to guess what somebody wants, I have to know the person. And I don't know you that well."

"Do you want to?"

Desire unwound and stretched lazily, deep in my belly.

"Look, what happened last night was…"

"Wild. Amazing."

"Irresponsible."

"I don't think so. We spent the night together because we wanted to. And it felt so good, so right that we forget that we are, in fact, strangers."

"Anything that starts so intense doesn't hold up for long. Don't you think it would be better to stop all this before getting hurt?"

"I don't want to. The intensity of what we felt the other night doesn't scare me, and I'm sure it doesn't scare you either."

It was so easy to succumb because, deep down, I wanted all that to be true.

"So, what do you say? Let's see where last night will take us," he said.

I imagined my life without him for a few seconds, and everything seemed black and white without colour. Did I want to give him up? Certainly not.

"All right," I said. "Let's see where last night will take us."

He released his held breath, relieved.

"I'll call when I get back to Miami. I'm presently in New York."

"What are you doing in New York?"

"I'm following up on some leads on a kidnapping case."

"How long will you stay?"

"I don't know how long it will take and if I'll be able to call you. I'm sure you understand the situation. I'll contact you when I can."

Hanging up, I leaned against my car, overwhelmed by the feelings that swamped me.

CHAPTER 14

The flight to Jacksonville was relatively smooth, and after an hour and twenty minutes, we rolled up to a beautiful, modern airport terminal. I like to have the ease of getting around the city without depending on cabs, and since renting a car was not in Moretti's budget, I decided to pay for it myself.

I followed the GPS instructions and pulled into the Jacksonville Police Department Homicide Unit parking lot twenty minutes later.

I stayed in my car waiting for Moretti's call until about nine. I was getting ready to call him when my phone buzzed, and the screen showed his number.

"Olsen," I said.

"I guess you're in Jacksonville," he answered, not bothering to say hello.

"I'm in the Jacksonville Police Department parking lot."

"Good. Go to the Homicide Division and ask for Lieutenant Morgan, William Morgen, who was part of the team that did the investigation. He's waiting for you."

I locked the car and walked inside the building, where

cops and criminals were already crowding. I approached the policeman at the counter, showed him my identification, and explained why I was there. He cocked his head at the telephone system and dialled a number.

"Lieutenant Morgen, a Detective Olsen here wants to talk to you."

He listened for a moment and then turned to me.

"He'll be with you in a minute."

The minute felt like an hour, and finally, a man emerged. He looked about fifty years old with a worn expression on his face.

He's seen too much on his job, I thought. He approached me and raised his head in surprise.

"Detective Olsen?" he asked.

"Yes, that's me," I said. "You look surprised."

He squinted his eyes as he scrutinized me.

"Well, I didn't expect somebody so … young. But I guess Moretti knows what he's doing. No offense."

"None taken."

He smiled and motioned for me to follow him into his office.

"Sit down," he said, moving around behind the desk and sitting in a swivel chair. He paused for a moment, and then he pulled a folder out of his file.

"This is all our evidence regarding the case," he said. "As you know, we never solved the case."

"Sergeant Moretti told me that you were part of the team that did the investigation. Please give me all your information about those crimes committed twenty years ago. I believe they are connected with those in Miami. It all points to the same offenders."

"What makes you think that?"

I took the report from my briefcase and handed it to him. He bent over the pages, studying them. After about five minutes, he looked up.

"I think you're right about the connection. But considering the intervals between kills, I guess it will be a long shot. However, to my knowledge, serial killers stay in one place, even in one neighbourhood."

"Not necessarily. Not if they are chasing something or someone specific."

"How do you know so much about serial killers?"

"I used to work for the FBI. Their training is more thorough than that of the police."

"Now I understand why Moretti gave you such a long leash. Did you ever see something similar to those crimes before?"

"Not like that, but close."

"Don't you find it challenging to do this job?"

"Because I'm a woman?"

"I didn't mean to offend you."

You keep repeating that, I thought.

"You didn't," I said instead.

"I suppose Moretti sent you here because he trusted your instincts."

"Not really. But he is desperate to find a culprit because his reputation is at stake."

"Hmm. You're very straightforward! I like you! I will try to help you with everything I know. This case and its baggage of memories and horrors made me doubt at the time if this was the job I was meant to do."

"Why?"

"I will tell you the whole story. Coffee?"

"Yes, thank you."

The coffee could have been better, but it would still meet the narrowest legal definition of the beverage.

"As you know," began Lieutenant Morgan, "forensics weren't advanced enough twenty years ago to develop a killer DNA profile. So, we focused on who the victims were, hoping that would help us narrow things down to identify who was responsible for the crimes.

"The case started growing and had a significant impact on the community. It created an atmosphere of fear.

"We had a lot of people calling in about people they thought were suspicious. We interviewed many people but found nothing that could lead us to believe they were the killers. We still didn't have that one piece of physical evidence that would link one of them to any of the cases. The constant thought was: what are we missing? In his desire to find the culprit, the sheriff had added more men to the case. A few months later, he began talking about the amount of money spent on the investigation and started cutting the task force. There was this belief that we wouldn't catch the killer, and we were always hoping that no one else would get killed.

"Time passed, and we didn't find anything conclusive, nothing to go on. The sheriff stopped the investigation. I was outraged."

I said, "Unfortunately, there are many cold cases in which the police are forced to stop the investigation due to a lack of evidence and budget. Emotions have no place in our profession."

"I know. But I was at the beginning of my career, and I knew one of the victims. He was forty years old, a father of two, and one of my neighbours. I thought that there was a killer out there who had come all the way, almost to my front door. The case was becoming an obsession for me. Whatever the reason, I couldn't seem to let go. How can we stop investigating with so many dead people?"

"I know the feeling," I said.

"Anyway, there was little I could have done about it."

He hesitated as if to say something more but decided not to.

"Something is eating away at you, making you evasive. Something you're not sure if you should tell me about."

"What makes you think that?"

"You told me the case was becoming like an obsession for you. I am led to believe that you have continued your investigation. At least, that is what I would have done."

"Well…" He let it hang for a moment. "You guessed right. I knew I would suffer the consequences if my boss knew what I was doing. Suspension, probably loss of pay. But I decided to take my chances."

"What happened?"

"During that time, we were called to a domestic dispute. When we arrived on site, we saw a woman beating the shit out of her husband. Watching her performance for a moment, I realized that, while I was looking for a man, a woman could very well be capable of committing a heinous crime. I started checking every detail I could find on the lives of the women involved in the case. It took me a short time to conclude that Nancy Connery could be a potential culprit."

"Who is Nancy Connery?"

"The last victim's wife, my neighbour. She worked for a Children's Charity Organization. She was beautiful, charming, knowledgeable and much loved in the neighbourhood. For some reason, I never liked her."

"What made you think she could have been the culprit?"

"First, the crimes started when she moved to Jacksonville from New York. Second, all the victims were donors to her charity."

"It could all have been pure coincidence," I said.

"Of course. I needed to find some evidence. But as I had minimal experience then, I decided it would be better to share my suspicions with my lieutenant. He was furious and ordered me to drop everything. To him, Nancy Connery was just a victim herself, devastated by the death of her husband.

Two weeks later, she had sold her house and returned to New York."

"So, you stopped investigating."

"I didn't have a choice. I was overwhelmed by the multitude of cases we were supposed to handle. Despite my obsession, I had to concentrate on the new cases, believing unreasonably, even stupidly, that there was an equal force opposing the force of evil and one day justice would be served."

"Why did you hesitate to tell me about your suspicions?"

"Because the more I thought about it, the more I concluded that Nancy Connery was innocent. We were looking for a sadistic person who had no regard for human life, and this person could not have been her. She dedicated her life to supporting abandoned and vulnerable children by collecting money for food, shelter, and education. I hesitated to share my suspicions with you because I don't want to influence your investigation and send you on a wild goose chase."

"You could be completely wrong about Nancy Connery. A sadistic psychopath could be someone who appears normal. It can be an upstanding member of society, entirely beyond suspicion in the light of day. He knows how to fit in."

"I'm still convinced she's innocent."

"Good to know. Can you think of anything else that might help me, any minor detail you forgot to mention?"

"I don't think I missed anything."

"If I can prove it is the same offenders in either case, would you consider reopening it?"

"Definitely."

He stood from his chair, letting me know our meeting was over.

CHAPTER 15

The ride back to the airport was pretty much the same as the ride in. It was past five o'clock when I got back to headquarters in Miami. Luckily, Moretti was closed up in the conference room, and nobody was at his desk. This would give me the time to see if Lieutenant Morgan's suspicions were founded and if Nancy Connery could be connected to the crimes.

I fired up my computer, and what I found left me gasping for breath: When Nancy Connery was seven years old, her father had been found guilty of killing several people and sentenced to life imprisonment, with no right of appeal. The police had found Nancy in the house basement, next to a dead body and stained with blood.

I closed my eyes and thought that criminals like Nancy Connery's father should not have children. If some roots are burrowed too deeply, they become harmful.

I took a deep breath and grabbed my mouse, eager to discover what happened to her. And there it was. After a few months spent in a psychiatric clinic, Nancy Connery was placed with a foster family.

But that was not all. It looked like bad luck was chasing her. A year and a half later, articles about the foster family that had taken her in were on every New York newspaper's front page. For years, the sadistic couple subjected the children to unimaginable abuse, torture, degradation, and psychological terror—until two children found the strength and courage to escape the nightmare and go to the police. One of these children was Nancy Connery.

Things were certainly getting interesting. When a child has such horrible experiences as Nancy, they can become a cold-blooded human predator.

I decided to print the articles that described the information and to be methodical; I pulled up the police records on Nancy Connery.

It wasn't much; she had no outstanding warrants, no special permits beyond a driver's license, and only a few parking tickets that she had paid. Her address was in Miami. She was the manager of Giving Hope, a children's charity organization.

With a bit of digging, I found one previous address in New York. Before that, she had lived in Jacksonville.

It remained to be seen if similar crimes had been committed in New York during her years there. Coincidence is always possible, but she could easily be a monster waiting to strike again. I grabbed my mousse and looked for the latest news on Nancy Connery in Miami.

The Giving Hope organization and its manager, Nancy Connery, organized numerous articles about charity events for children. The photos showed a woman in her fifties, still very attractive. She looked comfortable in front of the journalists' cameras, surrounded by influential people in Miami's political and economic life.

This meant that it would be challenging for the police to put her under surveillance without a valid reason.

From much experience, I knew you could get away with almost anything when you were a prominent figure. But it didn't matter to me. Nancy Connery may also be a predator, and nothing would stop me from finding out.

I picked up the printed articles and returned to my desk when I heard John's voice.

"Ah! Our team leader is back," he said.

"Don't be an asshole!" I fired back. "You must sort this out with him if you have a grudge against Moretti."

"Can't you see that the rules for me are completely different from yours? Do you know how much harder I have to work to get half the shit you take for granted? I did fucking everything to get that case. And he gives it to you like I don't even exist. You just don't see that."

"Because … I'm white?"

What other reason could he have? You've only been working with us for six months."

"Why didn't you think that he is desperate to settle this case because his reputation is at stake, and I have more experience in cases like this? When will you stop acting like a victim and behave like a cop?"

"It's easy for you to talk."

"Bullshit. That's total crap, and you know it. Your ego is playing with your head. But that's your problem."

At that moment, Maria Sanchez and Michael Bennett walked in.

"What do you have?" asked John.

"Nada," said Maria. "If all the cases are like this one, I won't stand a chance to become a detective."

"Luckily, they're not," said John.

"What about you, Liv?" asked Maria. "How did it go in Jacksonville? Tell us what you found."

I gave them a brief rundown about Lieutenant Morgan's obsession with the case and the suspicion that Nancy Connery may have been the culprit in the Jacksonville murders.

"It's hard to believe that a woman can be capable of such monstrous crimes!" said Michael.

"Maybe this is the reason she got away with murder," I said. "Everybody was looking for a man."

"What I meant is, is a woman strong enough to commit that kind of crime?" asked Michael.

"One of the most important features of the sadistic psychopath is that he is strikingly sure of himself in situations where others would tremble with sweat and fear," I said. "It gives him a lot of power over his victim."

"Still. We can't accuse Nancy Connery based solely on suspicions that Lieutenant Morgan had twenty years ago," said John.

"Of course not! But she may be connected to the crimes."

"What makes you believe that?"

I dropped the printed articles on his desk. He frowned. His eyes move up and down the pages a few times. Then he passed the copies to Maria and Michael.

"What do you think?" I asked them with impatience.

"Can violence be genetic?" asked Maria. "I know a little, but I never deepened my knowledge on this subject."

"You mean if Nancy's father was a criminal, could she have become one too?"

"Exactly."

"There is no psychopathy gene, but research tells us that psychopathy tends to run in families. Even if a parent does not have psychopathy, they may carry one or more genetic variants that increase their child's chance of developing psychopathy. People who have this neuropsychiatric disorder have a poor emotional response, lack of empathy, and poor behavioural controls, commonly resulting in persistent antisocial deviance and criminal behaviour."

"Which means that Nancy Connery can be one of them."

"She can be, yes. But we can't conclude that she is guilty only because it applies to her. Some psychiatrists work miracles with children like Nancy, who can become outstanding citizens. As you know, you have to prove someone's guilt."

"Of course," said John. "But after reading these articles and the police records, I agree that Nancy Connery can be considered a suspect. What do you think?" he asked Maria and Michael.

They both agreed that this was an avenue to pursue.

"All right, then. Let's write our reports and see if Moretti will buy it," I said.

By eight o'clock, I was saturated with coffee and impatient to see what Moretti would say about my suspicions about Nancy Connery. There was a faint sound of a throat clearing behind me, and when I turned around, I saw John standing there.

"Ready?"

I nodded, and we headed for Moretti's office. Maria and Michael were already there. Moretti gave us a tiny facial twitch that he probably thought was a warm smile.

"Ah, Detectives. It's about time."

I was ready to comment, but my phone rang, and I grabbed it.

"Olsen," I answered.

"Detective Olsen, my name is Gloria Perez. I have important information regarding Briana Cooper's killers."

I signalled the others to be quiet.

"Okay, Gloria. I'm listening."

"We can't do this over the phone. We need to meet."

"No problem. Where are you?"

"Meet me at the corner of Yellow and Lincoln streets in half an hour. Come alone."

"How do I recognize you?"

"Don't worry about it. Just be there."

"I will."

"We have a witness in Briana Cooper's crime," I explained to Moretti. "I'm going to get her."

"I'll go with you," said John.

"No. She wants me to go alone."

"Who is the witness?" I heard Moretti asking, but I was already rushing toward the exit.

CHAPTER 16

I scrambled down the stairs, hoping that Gloria Perez was not one of the many so-called witnesses who liked to play detective. And as I was approaching my car, I felt a tiny glimmer of hope blossom in my heart.

Traffic was light, and I arrived at the meeting place seven minutes early. I got out of the car and scanned the surroundings. An annoying and insistent electronic sound came from a club across the street.

The sidewalks were crowded with young people wearing minimal clothing, strolling rather than going anywhere, talking, singing, and drinking. None of them seemed in a hurry.

I wondered why Gloria Perez had chosen such a noisy place and if she was among those young people spilling in and out of the club. A crashing lightning bolt crossed the sky, and black clouds hid all possible moonlight. I felt someone's presence and a young girl approached me. She cleared her throat.

"You're Detective Olsen, right?"
I nodded. "That's right."

"I'm Gloria Perez."

She was barely nineteen years old. She was agitated, pacing in circles repeatedly; she was scared.

"Gloria, when you called me, you said you had important information regarding Briana Cooper's killers."

"I do. I saw the people who killed her. They've been following me. Maybe they are watching me right now."

"If they are, I won't let them get to you. But the best thing to do is to come with me to headquarters. One of our sketch artists will use your memory to reconstruct the killer's face and create a facial composite. A facial composite can help us identify criminals."

She looked at me for a moment, undecided about what to do.

"All right," she said at last. But I should tell my friends I'm leaving, or they'll get worried."

"Where are your friends?"

"Inside the club."

"I'll come with you."

"No. I don't think I'm in danger surrounded by so many people."

I wanted to tell her that, on the contrary, it was easy to commit a crime in a noisy club full of half-drunk people, but I didn't want to scare her more.

"All right, then. I'll wait for you here. But I'm coming inside if you're not back in ten minutes."

"I'll be back in five."

I took advantage of her absence to advise Moretti that we would need a sketch artist. Gloria was back in less than five minutes, and I drove quickly, moving smoothly in and out of traffic.

The sky was utterly dark, and heavy rain started falling when we arrived at headquarters. I asked Gloria to follow me. She walked quickly, with her head down, clearly preoccupied, and she didn't speak until we got inside. I signalled John to follow us into the interrogation room.

"Gloria, this is Detective John Freeman, my partner," I said.

"Hi, Gloria. Why don't you sit right here," said John, pointing to a chair. "You want some water?"

"No, thanks."

"Coffee?"

"No. I can't stay for long."

"We will have you out of here in no time," I assured her.

I wanted to ask her about Briana Cooper's killers right away, but I could see that she was very shaken up, and I wanted to give her the chance to compose herself.

"Gloria, how did you get my name and number?"

"I live in the neighbourhood where Mr. Miller was found dead. You questioned the neighbours, including my parents, if they saw anything suspicious. Your business card was on our dining room table. I took it."

"Why did you take so long to call me?"

"I was terrified."

"What were you terrified of?"

"The killers."

"Why?"

"Because they will kill me if they get wind that I talked to the police."

"Because you know them and what they did?" asked John.

"No. Because they know I saw them."

"Can you elaborate on this?"

"Of course. My cat took advantage of me when I left the door open by running away. I put on my sneakers, and I went looking for her. I was a few feet away from the house next door when the back door opened, and a man carrying a woman's body on his shoulder had come out. He was wearing a blood-stained plastic suit. Another man, dressed similarly but shorter, was holding the door open.

"I knew instantly that I was witnessing a crime, and I tried to wrestle down my panic, but it had me pinned to the ground, and my legs were shaking."

She stopped talking as if she had difficulty continuing.

"What happened next?" I asked her to bring her back to reality.

"The man carrying the woman's body looked straight into my eyes, and he slid his index finger across his throat, simulating what would happen to me if I did something stupid. I took a deep breath, took off across the garden as fast as possible, and didn't stop until I got to my room."

"Were you alone in the house?" I asked.

"No, with my brother and my parents."

"Are they aware of what happened?"

"No. I didn't want to worry them."

"Why didn't you call the police?" asked John.

"I was so shaken up that coming to my senses took a long time. By then, the killers were gone. I was afraid if they found out I called the police, they would get to me before the police found them. They knew where I lived."

"Did you get a good look at the killers?" asked John.

"Only the one who was carrying the body. His face will be etched in my memory forever. It's part of my nightmares."

"You said they were going out the back door. Was there a car parked nearby?"

"I didn't see any cars."

"Did you recognize the victim?"

"No, but when I saw Briana Cooper's picture on TV, I assumed she was the victim."

"What made you decide to call me?" I asked.

"I think I'm being followed."

"Followed? By whom?"

"By the killers. A car's been parked almost in front of my house for two days now."

"Always the same car?"

"Yes."

"Do they park in the same place?"

"No, but they're always positioned to have a view of the front door."

"Does the car follow you when you go out?"

"Yes. And then it parks near my school. You must think I'm paranoid."

"Not at all. It is only that stress can put all sorts of ideas in a person's head. I know a lot about that."

"Believe me. It's not the stress."

"Didn't you think about writing down the license plate number?" asked John.

"Of course! I thought about it but was afraid to get too close."

"Do you know the make of the car?"

"I could be better at recognizing car brands. It's a black SUV."

"Is there anything else, any small detail you can tell me?" I asked.

"No. How much longer do I have to stay?"

"We're nearly done. I'll leave you with John and see if our sketch artist has arrived."

I barely managed to stand up when the door opened, and Peter MacDonald, one of our sketch artists, walked in. Moretti, who had followed the whole process on the department computer, had managed to get Peter here in record time.

"Gloria, this is Peter, our sketch artist," I told her.

"Hello, Gloria," said Peter with a small smile. "Why don't you start by describing the face of the offender?"

By the time Peter was done, I could barely contain my

impatience.

"That's the best I can do," he finally said, leaving the interrogation room.

I looked at the facial composite and wasn't shocked to recognize Robert Wilson, the attorney of Sunshine Build Group. I knew the killer must be smart enough to commit such a perfect crime and eventually knew the Millers.

"Detective Olsen, you're not going to tell me if you recognized the suspect?" asked Gloria.

"I'm sorry, Gloria, but I can't tell you that."

"You don't have to worry about him anymore," John added. "We will protect you."

I signalled John to step outside and told him I recognized Robert Wilson in the facial composite.

"Are you sure?"

"I'm telling you, it's him. Inform Moretti to make the identification and make sure there is a patrol car to take Gloria home and that she will be under surveillance until we arrest the killers."

A half-hour later, I asked Gloria to follow me to the parking lot, where a patrol car was waiting to take her home.

CHAPTER 17

When I got back inside, it was excellent news all around. I barely closed the door when Moretti cleared his throat, getting everyone's attention.

"Oh right, listen up. Now that we have the identity of one of the culprits and his home address, we must act immediately before he disappears. It's going to be a long night. Call your wives, husbands, your girlfriends, and your boyfriends. No one leaves until we arrest him and bring him here. I will detour to get a warrant and meet you there. Let's move it."

We put on Kevlar vests, and the instant Maria and Michael drove away from headquarters, we followed them.

"It looks like we were wrong to suspect Nancy Connery," said John.

"I still think she's somehow connected to those crimes," I said. "But in the meantime, let's concentrate on what we've got."

We stopped a little distance from Robert Wilson's house to wait for Moretti. He arrived almost simultaneously with the investigation team, who were supposed to focus heavily on gathering evidence that may prove Robert Wilson's guilt. He split the team to secure all the exits from the house.

"You two, take the front door," he ordered, addressing myself and John. "And stay sharp. This guy could be dangerous. Go."

We ran almost noiselessly to Robert Wilson's house and took our positions. John knocked on the door.

"This is the police," he said. "Open the door."

After several knocks, Robert Wilson appeared in the doorway.

"Step out here, please," John ordered.

"Why?"

"Nice and slow. Move out of the house," insisted John.

"What's this about?"

"Are you Robert Wilson?"

"Why, what the hell is this about?"

"Sir, please answer the question," replied John. "Are you Robert Wilson?"

"Yes, I am."

"We have a warrant for your arrest."

"What?"

"Don't move. Show me your hands."

"Okay, okay," Wilson said.

I went over and put the cuffs on him.

"Robert Wilson, I'm arresting you for the murder of Briana Cooper. You have the right to remain silent. Anything you say can and will be used against you in court. You have the right to…"

He let me finish explaining his rights, harbouring a smile on his face.

"You're making a big mistake," he said. "I have no idea who Briana Cooper is."

"Then you have nothing to worry about," I answered.

"Let's go."

By the time we got back to headquarters, it was 11:45 p.m. It had been a rough day for everyone. We headed down the hall to one of the interrogation rooms and started the questioning.

John began the recording: "Robert Wilson at 11:55 p.m.," he stated, indicating the date, time and place, as well as our names as present detectives.

"Okay, so you know why you're here, Mr. Wilson?" John asked.

"I believe, by mistake."

"Do you know this woman?" I asked, showing him the photo of Briana Cooper.

"No."

There was no change in his facial expression.

"You've never seen her before?"

"Never."

"Do you know who did that to her?" John asked.

"The answer to your question is no. I don't have a clue."

"Look at it again," I insisted. "Did you do that to her, Mr. Wilson? Did you enjoy stabbing her to death?"

"That's what I call all crap. If I want to kill someone, why don't I use a gun? It's easier and faster to get rid of someone with a bullet than a knife."

"Knives are silent," I said. "And they give you the ability to dehumanize your victims. It's about power, control, and the thrill. Isn't that what you were looking for when you killed her?"

He stood up. "I'd like to leave now."

"Please sit down, Mr. Wilson."

"I'm done with your questions. You don't have any proof against me."

I decided to push him off-balance.

"Don't we? How about this?"

I showed him the facial composite.

"We have a witness who places you at the crime scene."

An icy, unpleasant look appeared in his eyes, immediately replaced by a half-smile.

"It means nothing," he said, completely controlling his emotions. "There are many people out there who look like me."

"This is a homicide investigation, Mr. Wilson. Do you understand how serious it is?" I asked.

"As a lawyer, I think I do."

"Where were you Monday between four and five?" asked John.

Wilson took a moment to consider.

"I was in court."

"What about between eight and midnight?" I intervened.

I saw a tiny flicker of surprise on his face.

"Are you accusing me of killing Harry Miller, too?

"How do you know what time Harry Miller was killed?"

"Because it was all over the news. I'm telling you, I've got nothing to do with any murder."

"You didn't answer my question. Where were you Monday between eight and midnight?" I insisted.

"I was at the French Riviera restaurant."

"Alone?"

"With my girlfriend."

"What is your girlfriend's name?"

"Olivia Mansfield. She is a lawyer as well."

"We need her contact information."

"Of course."

"What time did you leave the restaurant?"

"Around ten-thirty. Look, I'm not a criminal. This interrogation is insulting and a waste of time. I'm done here."

"Mr. Wilson, you're a lawyer, aren't you?" I asked.

"Last I checked, yeah."

"Then you know we have sufficient evidence for your arrest. Remember, the evidence doesn't have to show guilt beyond a reasonable doubt until trial."

"You mean I'll be tried for murder?"

"Unless you have an alibi that proves your innocence."

At that moment, the door opened, and Sergeant Moretti beckoned me to follow him. I stood up and walked out of the room. Moretti turned to face me.

"It's getting late. I don't think this guy is going to talk. Complete the interrogation."

"My instinct tells me that Robert Wilson is guilty," I protested.

"We cannot rely on your gut instinct. Complete the interrogation."

"But we have a witness who recognizes him as the culprit!"

"I agree. And that's why I'll keep him here until tomorrow when we check his alibi. But if he's telling the truth, we will have no choice but to let him go."

I knew better than to argue with him. Moretti was a very ambitious man. Undoubtedly, he considered this case a launching pad for promotion. Or, conversely, a crash landing if he blew it.

I went inside and leaned over to John to tell him about Moretti's decision. John shrugged his shoulders and declared the interrogation over. Then he stood up and walked out of the room. I followed. We joined Maria and Michael, who had observed the questioning through a one-way mirror. They looked tired.

"Try to look at the bright side," said Maria, addressing John and me. "If Gloria Perez agrees to testify in court and identifies him as a criminal, it doesn't matter that he's a lawyer."

"She's right," said Moretti. "Good job, everybody! It's

been a very long day, and we all need a few hours of rest. Go home."

But for some reason, his praise did not lighten my mood.

CHAPTER 18

I did not sleep well that night. I stayed for a long time on the terrace, listening to the wind coming hard from the ocean, carrying some hint of the rain that had just stopped. Fortunately, the hurricane had spared the city of Miami and headed toward the Carolinas with force. My thoughts were consumed by the murders, by the fact that I saw people's lives change forever, for the worse, every day.

It's part of the job, my father used to say. *Finding the bad guy, finding justice. We owe it to the living and the dead.*

Would I find the bad guys this time?

I rolled between the sheets for most of the night until, eventually, fatigue got the better of me. The following day, I was awakened by heavy rain crashing against the windows.

Even though it was Saturday and there wasn't much traffic, it took me longer than usual to get to work.

The sky was tar-black, and puddles began plinking as the rainfall became heavier. The roofs of the cars danced with spray, and I could hear the murmuring of the rain through the window. It sounded like the buzzing of angry bees.

I had just settled dawn with a cup of coffee, ready to

watch the interview recording of Robert Wilson, when Moretti poked his head in the door.

"Did you see this? I had the journalists blowing up my phone all morning."

He threw a newspaper on my desk. Gloria Perez's picture was on the front page, below the title: *"Witness in crimes?"*

"Do you have any idea who leaked the information to the press? Do you have something to do with that?"

"You're questioning my integrity," I replied, feeling insulted. "You know I couldn't do that!"

"Maybe you wanted to make yourself famous."

"This has nothing to do with me! Perhaps you leaked the information to the press to prove you had not lost control of the situation."

"If you wish to continue working here, you must keep those emotions in check. Find Gloria Perez and bring her here. I want her to see Robert Wilson in person and confirm that he is one of the two killers."

"You said you'd keep her under watch. Why not ask the surveillance guys to bring her in?"

"Look, I don't have money to watch innocent people."

"What do you mean by that?"

"Gloria Perez's house was under watch all night, and nothing happened. Maybe nobody is following her, and it's just her imagination. I removed the watch this morning."

"And now her life is in danger!"

"All right, point made. Now go and bring Gloria Perez in."

Before I could open my mouth, he was gone. I called Gloria's phone number, but I got her voicemail.

"Hi, this is Gloria…"

"Hi, Gloria, this is Detective Liv Olsen. I need to talk to you. Please call me back."

I had only taken a few steps down the hall when my

phone rang.

"Olsen."

"It's me, Gloria. I'm in trouble, and I don't see any policemen. You promised me that the police would protect me."

"Where are you?"

"I'm at the entrance to Greenfield Park. I'm sure somebody is following me."

"Stay where you are. I will be there soon."

I dialled John's number.

"Freeman."

"John, I just spoke to Gloria. She's in trouble. She's sure somebody is following her."

"What about the surveillance?"

"There is no surveillance. I'll explain later. She's at the entrance to Greenfield Park. I'm heading there now."

"All right. I will advise the nearest park patrol."

I called Gloria back.

"Gloria, we will send the nearest patrol to your location. And I will be there very soon."

"I left that location," she told me. "The person who was following me was getting too close. I was scared."

"Where are you now?"

"In the park."

"No! Get out of the park. Get among people, okay?"

"Okay. I'm going back on the street. There's a shopping mall across the street. I'll wait for you inside."

"All right. I'm heading there now. Call me when you get inside the mall."

The traffic had gotten a little thicker, even though the sky was even darker and clouds filled with water announced the approach of heavy rain. By now, Gloria should have arrived at the mall. So why wasn't she calling me? I dialled her number, and it went to voicemail.

"Gloria, did you get inside the mall? Call me."

Minutes passed, and my phone remained silent. I redialed her number.

"Gloria, it's Detective Olsen again. I need to know that you're okay. Please call me back."

The rain started pouring down heavily, slowing down the traffic. I stared at the phone for a long moment before deciding what to do next, and then I dialled John's number.

"John, have you heard from the police patrol?"

"Yes, I was just about to call you. They didn't find Gloria."

"Because she's no longer there. She's trying to get to the mall. You should send them there."

"I will. Tell Gloria they will be there soon."

"She doesn't answer my calls anymore. I think her life is in danger. We have to track her phone."

"We need to get a court order for the trace. That will take some time."

"We don't have the time. Until then, Gloria may be dead. Go talk to Lee."

"I can't do this without Moretti's permission, you know that."

"You have to talk to Moretti right away. He's the one who put Gloria's life in danger by cancelling the surveillance."

Five minutes later, he called me back.

"Lee's tracking Gloria's phone. Call him to get directions."

Lee answered right away.

"Lee, this is Liv. I need the trace now."

"Just gaining access. I'm nearly there … okay … Gloria's not in the mall. You have to drive north. The exact location should be on your car console now."

I suddenly accelerated into the left lane and turned left across oncoming traffic, blasting the siren. I reached where Gloria was supposed to be, but she was nowhere to be seen.

"Lee, are you sure this is the right location? There's no

one here.”

“Of course, I’m sure! She’s right there.”

I cut the engine, stepped out of the car, and dialled Gloria’s number. It took me a moment to hear the ringing over the thumping of the rain. For a moment, I froze in place, knowing what it meant. I picked up Gloria’s phone, thinking the devil had won again.

I circled for a while, hoping I was not too late to save Gloria, when my phone began to chirp.

“Olsen.”

“Did you find Gloria?” asked Lee in a worried voice.

“No. Just her phone. You have to notify Moretti. I need help.”

“That’s not good. The patrols found a dead body two blocks from where you are. Moretti and the team are on their way there.”

“What do you mean? What body? I didn’t get anything from dispatch!”

“Hold on. I’ll transfer you to John.”

A few seconds later, I heard John’s voice.

“Hello, Liv. We have a dead person on Fillmore Street. We’re heading there right now.”

“I’m on my way.”

As I turned onto Fillmore Street, I saw a group of people standing in the rain around the yellow tape that the police had installed. I showed my credentials to one of the two police officers who was present, and I approached the body lying on the sidewalk.

For an endless moment, I stood there looking down at Gloria’s lifeless body. Her face was pale and set in an expression of weary terror. Death did not fit her, not someone so young. It wasn’t right. It wasn’t fair.

I started looking around, trying to find something that would give me a clue as to who the killer might be, when I heard the sirens of several police cars. My team had arrived.

"What have we got?" asked Moretti.

"We have a young girl who died because you decided she did not deserve to be under surveillance," I accused him.

He looked at me, then looked away, and then down at his feet.

"What do you want me to say?" he answered, his voice rich with irritation.

"It's your fault that this girl is dead. And nothing you can say will bring her back to life."

He muttered something I didn't catch and signalled the two police officers to come closer.

"Who called it in?" he asked them.

"I did," replied one of them. "We were on routine patrol when we saw this young lady lying on the sidewalk. Her body was still warm."

"Have you noticed anything that can help us find who did this?"

"I spotted a black Toyota Highlander parked nearby. But before arriving at the point where I could visualize the interior, the car left its location. Although I sprinted forward, the first letters were the most I could see on the license plate. Here it is."

He took a paper out of his pocket and gave it to Moretti.

"Good job!" said Moretti.

I expected him to share the information with me, but instead, he took out his phone and walked toward his car.

I turned around and saw Philippe on one knee, just finishing an examination of a probable footprint.

"Hey, Philippe. Have you got something?" I asked.

"Not much. Before we arrived, these two patrol guys dragged around all over every grass blade. And the rain is not helping."

I stepped around Philippe to where Tom was meticulously

flashing his camera. Despite the gusty rain, there was still a surprising amount of blood, and Tom focused his camera on every drop.

"How did she die, Tom?" I asked.

"She's got a stab wound through the neck. Whoever stabbed her perfectly severed her carotid. This spray," he said, pointing to the blood trails on the nearest tree, "is from her last heartbeats. You only get that force and volume with a total arterial transection. It's impressive."

"What do you mean?"

"Well … considering the perfection of the cut, the killer is a professional. "

"I'll say he's a monster."

"That too."

I looked down at Gloria's dead body. I had been on the scene of many homicides, but I never felt the anger and guilt I was feeling now.

"Gary," I said to the medical examiner. "I don't see any defensive wounds!"

"Because there are no defensive wounds. Just as in the Miller family cases."

"It doesn't make sense. Gloria knew someone was after her. She didn't seem like someone who would go down without a fight. She dared to come to the police even though she knew she was putting her life at risk."

"I will say that she did not have the chance to defend herself. Not with a perfectly severed carotid."

"Can you tell me more?"

"I'll tell you more after I perform the autopsy."

I felt the steady rain pouring into my clothing, the helplessness flooding in. I needed to find a clue as much as an asthmatic needs air, and yet I had nothing but dead people.

CHAPTER 19

There was nothing more to do for us at the crime scene. Tom, Philippe, and the other forensic nerds would spot everything worth the trouble. Maria had dug up a videotape from a camera across the street, and we hoped it covered the spot where Gloria Perez had lost her life.

"Oh right," said Moretti. "Listen up. The two police officers who discovered the body took the first letters of the license plate number of a Toyota Highlander that was parked suspiciously close to the place where Gloria Perez was killed. Wang is trying to find the registration as we speak. We might have some small bit of luck. I'll let you know as soon as the car is found. Maybe…"

His telephone started buzzing.

"Wait a second," he said, fumbling his phone out of his pocket.

"Moretti … okay, I'll be there."

He shook his head and cleared his throat.

"Goddamn it," he said, addressing us all. "We have another dead body. Let's go."

The fact that he wanted John and me to go too infuriated

me. We'd never be able to find the sadistic psychopaths that had terrorized the city if he wanted us at every crime scene.

"What's going on?" exclaimed John. "They've all gone; let's go if you don't want us to be the last."

"Doesn't it bother you that Moretti won't give us time to settle our case?"

"Maybe he's hoping there's a connection with this new case and wants us present. Maybe we'll find enough evidence to catch the killers this time."

"Or maybe not."

We drove along in silence, each lost in his thoughts. When we got to the crime scene, the rain became heavier. The body was lying in the entrance hall of a house under demolition. I went down on one knee beside Gary, the medical examiner.

"What can you tell me, Gary?"

"Male, early 50s. The demolition crew discovered his body two hours ago. He's been dead for at least fourteen hours. Found this in his back pocket."

"It looks like a hotel swipe card."

"That's all he had on him, no ID, no keys, no phone. So far, we're talking John Doe."

"Well dressed," I said.

"Well stabbed, too. Multiple penetrative wounds. He lost a lot of blood."

"Someone was trying to make him suffer."

"Could be. Or someone who realizes how long it takes to stab someone to death."

"What do you mean?"

"Compared to the Gloria Perez killer, this one is a novice. I think this guy was still alive when the killer left the scene. And then he dragged himself this way toward the entrance."

"No phone, no one around to hear him; he didn't stand a chance," John said.

"That's right," Gary confirmed.

"What's underneath that fingernail, Gary?" I asked him, fighting to keep the eagerness out of my voice.

"Looks like the victim took some hair with him," Gary said, removing the hair with a tweezer.

"Which means he put up a fight."

"Exactly. The good news is, he got a follicular tag."

Gary put the hair in a small plastic bag, which he handed to Philippe.

"Let's go see if the neighbours have seen or heard anything," John said, motioning me to follow him.

With the rain falling so hard, we were not surprised that no one was in sight.

We spent the next hour and a half questioning the neighbours, who seemed genuinely surprised that somebody had committed a crime in their neighbourhood. They were staring at us with dismay, bordering on shock.

By the time we finished questioning them, our team was wrapping up. We followed Tom to the lab and waited for him to run the test on the victim's blood.

His name was Alejandro Martinez, just twenty-seven, but he had already been booked for possession, assault, and solicitation.

"That's a hard life," said John.

"And an even harder death," I concluded. "Let's see if Philippe is still waiting on the DNA result on the hair from under the victim's nails."

We found Philippe watching the Identifications System screen, hoping for a match. The chirping of the system stopped, and we heard him exclaim, "Ah! A familiar face: Juan Garcia. He's connected with the Colombian cartel. He was convicted of drug trafficking and was released on probation three months ago."

"Do we have an address?"

"Let's see … here it is."

"Thanks, Philippe," John said.

"Get the SWAT," said Philippe with concern in his voice. "This guy is very dangerous."

"No worries," said John. "We are also dangerous."

Two hours later, we had Juan Garcia in the interrogation room.

"Mr. Garcia, do you know a guy named Alejandro Martinez?" I asked.

"No. I don't know a guy by that name. I'm sorry."

I showed him the picture of the victim.

"As I said, I don't know him," insisted Garcia.

"You've never see him before?"

"Never."

"This man was found dead this morning."

"His death has nothing to do with me."

"We found hair under his fingernails, Mr. Garcia. And the problem is that the DNA profile matches yours."

"How can that be possible?!"

"Why don't you tell us?"

"I see that you are not listening to me! I've been at the theatre all evening. Two movies, back to back."

He pulled out cinema tickets.

"Can anyone vouch for that?"

"No. I went alone."

"That's a hell of an alibi," said John.

"What do you mean?"

"You know what an alibi is, Mr. Garcia?"

"I do!"

"Good, because you don't have one," said John.

He turned to the officer standing by the door.

"Cuff him."

"I won't be here for long," said Garcia with a sly smile.

The officer pushed him toward the door, giving him no time to make further remarks.

"He may be right when he's saying he won't be here for long," said John. "The Colombian cartel is powerful here in Miami. They have some excellent lawyers."

"It all depends on how important he is to the cartel," I said. "And don't forget that we have hard evidence against him."

"You're right. Let's order something to eat. I'm starving."

"Why don't you order while I see if Philippe has anything for us in Gloria's case."

"What would you like to eat?"

"A salad: lettuce, avocado, carrots, and a boiled egg."

"A salad! What about a large pizza?"

"You can order it for yourself."

I headed to the lab and found Philippe staring at something under a microscope.

"Hey, Philippe. Did you find anything on Gloria's killer?"

"Nothing. The crime was committed with the same control as in Miller's case. "

"What about the footprints?"

"Because of the rain, we only have partials. But I'm trying something different that might help narrow your investigation."

"What is it?"

"It's called stature analysis. The laser creates a 3-D representation of the print. The computer then measures the depth of the impressions of the heel, ball, and toes. I can input those measurements, giving us the person's weight and height. We should have the results any minute," he said, motioning me to follow him in front of a chirping computer.

I wondered how far forensics had come with the computer when my cellphone rang. It was Jensen.

It was the first time he called me since he left for New York.

"I have to take this," I told Philippe and left the lab.

"Hello, Jensen," I said.

"I miss you," he whispered.

I felt my blood pumping faster in my veins.

"Me, too. When are you coming back?"

"I'm not sure yet. This case is taking longer than I expected."

The laboratory door opened, and Philippe signalled that he had the analysis results.

"Sorry, Jensen, I'll have to let you go; I'm in the middle of an investigation."

"It's okay. I just wanted to hear your voice."

Shaking my head to clear my thoughts, I headed into the lab. The computer wasn't chirping, and Philippe beckoned me to come closer.

"There," he said, pointing toward the monitor. "Whoever wore these shoes is between six feet and six feet one inch tall."

"Can you compare this data with what was found at Briana Cooper's and the Millers' crime scenes?"

"Of course. Let's see…"

The computer started chirping, and a few seconds later, we had a match.

"There you go," said Philippe. "It confirms the footprint belongs to one of the two killers."

"And they're always one step ahead of us," I said.

Philippe shook his head.

"Look. I share your frustration, but I have nothing else to work with. This … or those killers are intelligent and extremely careful. It's a clean job. I'll do more digging tomorrow."

I looked at my watch; the time was six twenty-eight. I didn't realize it had gotten so late.

"Thank you, Philippe," I said and left the lab.

I found John sharing an extra-large pizza with Maria Sanchez and Michael Bennett at his desk.

"Here's your salad," he said, swallowing the last piece of pizza. "Judging by your expression, Philippe has no new evidence in the case," he guessed.

"No, he only confirmed what we already suspected; the footprints match those found at the Briana Cooper and Miller crime scenes," I replied.

"What about the video capture from the traffic camera that Maria has found?" I asked.

"Nothing in it," said Maria. "It didn't cover the perimeter where the crime happened. We have no clues, no suspects, and the only witness is dead."

"Unless there is a connection between the car that the patrol officer found suspicious and the crime," said Michael. "Lee is looking right now in the database for automobile registration."

"Good luck with that," replied John. "Do you know how many Toyota Highlanders are registered in Miami? Hundreds."

"What…" exclaimed Maria. "We've got to go through all of them?"

"No, dummy! We aren't doing anything," said John. "Lee will do all the work, and we will question the owners of the cars he finds suspicious!"

"Okay, smart ass! Let's hope that Lee will work some magic."

"What if this is just a case we can't solve?" Michael said, his voice heavy with frustration.

"Why are you saying that?" I asked him.

He sighed, his gaze fixed on the evidence board covered in gruesome crime scene photos.

"Well, I mean, there are plenty of homicide departments out there with piles of unsolved cases like this one. If Lee finds nothing, we're at a dead end."

"Lee is the best at what he does," I replied, trying to reassure all of us. "We have to be patient."

"I hope we don't have to wait all night," Michael grumbled. "Some of us like to sleep from time to time."

Maria chimed in with a smirk, "Tell that to Moretti."

"Let's recap everything," interrupted John. "Maybe we missed a detail."

Despite his exhaustion, Michael managed a weak smile.

"That's a good idea," he admitted. "That's what I was going to suggest."

Deep down, I couldn't help but acknowledge my own doubts. As much as I hated to admit it, finding a breakthrough in this case was becoming increasingly elusive.

CHAPTER 20

It was eight forty-five before Moretti finally made his appearance. He looked tired.

"Wang is still checking out suspicious cars," he explained. "Tomorrow morning, I'll send people to eliminate those with an alibi. Anything to report?" he asked.

"No real progress yet," I said. "The only thing we have are footprints that match those found at the Miller and Cooper crime scenes."

"That's not enough to find a freaking serial killer. I want more."

"We still have Robert Wilson in custody. We should check his footprints," I suggested.

He blinked and stared at me.

"We will. But I don't think it will get us anywhere. Robert Wilson seemed innocent to me during the interrogation. And he has a solid alibi."

"Then why is he still here?" I asked. "His fiancée is a lawyer; she should have proved his alibi by now!"

"The fact that he was in our custody while Gloria Perez got killed proves his innocence," Moretti thundered.

"Or, perhaps, that's why he wasn't in a hurry to show us his alibi," I insisted. "By killing Gloria, his partner in crime was clearing a path for him."

He shook his head, looking annoyed.

"I started wondering about your competence, Detective Olsen," he said with an edge of sarcasm. "Except for speculation and gut instinct, I didn't get much from you."

I could see the muscles flexing along his face and shoulders. It was pointless to say something. He trailed off and looked around the room.

"All right then," he said, "we're done for tonight."

He squared his shoulders and left the room.

"Jesus! He cannot refrain from doing this!" said Maria, rolling her eyes.

"Doing what?" asked Michael.

"He has to take out his frustration on someone."

"Yeah…" I said. "I think that's the best part of Moretti's day."

"Do you really think Robert Wilson is guilty?" Maria asked me.

Her eyes scanned my face as if she wanted to see if I hid something I didn't want to reveal.

"We could not dismiss the possibility," I said. "There is something dark and wicked about Robert Wilson."

"Well, that was a long day," said Michael. "We deserve a drink. What are you saying?"

"Earlier, you were complaining that you were tired!" John exclaimed.

"I am. But listening to music and having a drink surrounded by happy tourists will help me sleep better than going to bed stressed."

"Well then, let's go," said an enthusiastic Maria.

"I prefer to spend some time with my son," concluded John.

"What about you? "Maria asked me.

"Not tonight; I'm too tired," I answered, not feeling like going.

"Well, then, I guess it's me and you," she said, addressing Michael.

I walked with them to the parking lot. The rain had stopped, and the moon was bright, its rays bouncing off the dark water of the sea. I tried to lean back and enjoy the ride but couldn't.

I was halfway toward home when I slammed on the brakes, propelling the car into the shoulder of the road. Neither my mind nor my body was at ease. The events of the last few days were spinning in my head. There was no question of being able to sleep.

I turned the car around and headed for the gym, where I could satisfy an increasing urge to throw a few punches to release all the anger I was carrying in my body.

Usually, the gym is filled with a crowd of people who come to train in mixed martial arts. Some train for competitions, while others prepare to learn self-defence techniques.

Mike Harris, the owner of the gym and a former MMA champion, thought I was very talented and tried to convince me to quit my job and train seriously for competition.

"Come on, Liv! You can take anyone," he would say.

But his passion wasn't mine. The reason my father trained me since I was seven years old had nothing to do with competitions.

As I walked into the training room, Mike motioned me to come closer.

"Liv! I'm glad you came. I have a challenge for you," he said solemnly.

"Who?"

"A new member. He's from Brazil. Get changed while I clear a ring."

I changed and saw Mike in the middle of the room, next to a boxing ring. I approached and climbed over the ropes.

"Okay. Let's warm you up," Mike said. "I'll try to go easy on you because your opponent will be relentless. He will be furious that I make him fight against a woman."

"Then why are you doing it?"

"He's a good fighter, but he is too arrogant. Arrogance has no place in a competition. Let's give him a lesson."

After the first warm-up phase, Mike changed his tactics.

"Nice!" he said. "Top, top. Watch the scramble."

I could feel my body following his instructions with ease.

"Beautiful! There it is!"

After half an hour, my body and mind were prepared for the challenge.

"All right," said Mike. "You're ready."

He turned to one of the men who had approached the ring during my warm-up and motioned for him to come closer. His muscle mass was incredible. A smirk appeared on his lips as he stepped into the ring as if to tell me I was crazy to fight against him.

Maybe he was right, but after all, I was there to release some tension.

"Liv, this is Gustavo," said Mike. "He wants to become the next MMA champion."

"I will never be a champion if you make me train with women," said Gustavo. Mike was right; Gustavo was quite arrogant.

"All right, let's see it," said Mike, ignoring Gustavo's remark. "Go."

"If your opponent is stronger physically, don't wait," my father used to tell me. "Go in. Move first. Distract. Take control."

And that is precisely what I did. I moved so fast that Gustavo didn't even see the hits coming. They rained down on his face and body like bolts of lightning.

"All right," said Mike. "Hooks in. Get it. Pick your shots."

Gustavo was trying to stop the flurry of kicks without succeeding. His breathing was heavy, and half of his jaw was beginning to bruise.

"Beautiful!" said Mike. "Hold … hold … break!"

Gustavo swayed so severely that he had to hold on to the ropes for support.

"All right," said Mike, motioning with his hand for us to return to the center of the ring.

A flying knee hit me right in the stomach, and another landed on my ribs. I ducked to evade another kick. Gustavo was aiming for my face.

"I'll finish you off," he snarled.

"C'mon Liv!" yelled Mike. "Open him up. You got it. Lock it in."

Gustavo charged at me headfirst and grabbed my waist, but lifting me proved harder than expected. The fact that he could not overpower me had triggered an eruption of violence, and he was losing control of himself.

He tried to hit my windpipe, an illegal action in an MMA competition. I broke free and wrapped my legs around his neck, and before he knew what was happening, he was on the floor.

He tried to free himself but couldn't while I tightened my grip. I could almost feel his bones changing shape. He was lying on the floor gasping for air, surprised by my strength. When I thought I could no longer keep my grip, he started tapping with his hand to notify me of his submission.

The people around the ring started to applaud my victory while Mike looked at me with a satisfied smile. He took a step toward Gustavo and cleared his throat.

"Gustavo, you tried to subdue Liv with an intentional throat punch! No direct throat strikes are allowed in MMA competitions. That's manslaughter. You only need that move if you believe your life is in danger."

"Sorry, I got carried away…"

I let them talk, picked up my gym bag, and headed for the exit. I felt exhausted and needed a shower. It was time to go home.

CHAPTER 21

The car's door swung open, and the man I was waiting for slid behind the wheel. I was seated on the passenger side before he put the key in the ignition and started the car.

"Who the hell are you?" he exclaimed.

"Drive," I said.

"Fuck you! Get out of my car!"

I took the gun out of my pocket and pointed it toward him. That was enough to make him behave.

"Where are we going?" he asked.

"Just drive, and do not talk. I'll give you the directions."

He put the car in gear and drove. If anything, traffic was getting worse by the minute. People were becoming impatient and hated everyone who wanted to take their places. It was a delightful mixture of rage and hostility, cheering me up immensely. Compared to them, I was in complete control of my emotions.

I closed my eyes momentarily, imagining what I would do to the man driving. By that point, he should have been dead scared, and his fear would grow, rising into panic and, at last, full-fledged terror.

I felt a small surge of hot anticipation. I looked at the cars around me and let myself soak in the delicious feeling of anonymous, ultimate power.

I was wrapped up in my pleasant daydreams when I realized we were a few blocks from the house. I scanned the area for anyone watching, but all was as peaceful and unsuspecting as I wanted. Everything was going according to plan.

I climbed out of the car as soon as we got inside the garage.

"Out! Quickly!" I hissed at the main inside, holding the gun in the ready position. "Don't try something foolish, or I'll kill you. Do you understand?"

"I understand," he answered, not taking his eyes off the gun.

I took him inside the house where my mother was waiting for us.

"Nicely done, my mother said. All clear?"

"So it would seem," I answered.

"For Christ's sake! Who the hell are you people?" the man exclaimed. "What do you want from me?"

I pressed the gun to the back of his neck.

"Relax!" I said. "Everything will be over soon."

"That's very reassuring," he said.

He fell silent. A tremendous thrill ran through me while I bound his hands with tape. His eyes widened, and he dropped to his knees, begging us to let him go.

We watched him for a moment, letting his fear grow, allowing the joy of our pleasure to fulfill us.

"Please," he whispered again, his body shaking hard. "If this is about the money I owe, I promise I will pay till the last penny."

But we had no intention of stopping. An electric surge was rising inside us, from the base of our spines to the tops of our heads. We silenced him, dragged him into the bathroom, and put him in the tub. He saw the knife in my hand, and his muscles knotted against the duct tape, his breath hissing in for a scream that would never get past the gag.

We stopped momentarily to enjoy the delicious taste of his terror and then went to work.

I slashed his body with precise movements, making neat and clean cuts until I felt the approach of fulfillment. I put down the knife and looked at my mother, needing her to approve of the perfection of the crime I had just committed. She seemed to be in a state of deep contentment.

"This is who we are," she finally said. "We have the power to decide who lives and who dies."

CHAPTER 22

Rush hour was in full swing as I headed to work, and the traffic was snarled beyond repair. The rain was long gone, and the streets were already dry and filled with cars. Following an accident, the police stopped the traffic, and it took me half an hour longer than usual to get to work.

"Where the goddamn hell have you been?" asked John as soon as I stepped inside the station.

"Good morning, John. Traffic was a bitch," I answered.

"Moretti keeps asking about you. He told me to fetch you as soon as you get in."

"All right, then. Let's go see what Moretti wants."

As we opened the door to his office, Moretti stood up from his desk and stretched his back.

"Detective Olsen! You have finally decided to honour us with your presence."

"Sorry, Sergeant, but the traffic..."

He made a sign with his hand: spare me the details.

"Wang worked most of the night," he said. "The number of suspected Toyota Highlanders came down to seven."

"Nice!" said John. "Do you want us to go and verify the

owners' alibis?"

"No. I already sent people to check their alibis. Let's wait and see the results."

"What do you want us to do?"

"I asked the officers to take Robert Wilson to the interrogation room. Let's see what you can get out of him."

We followed him down the hall, surprised by his decision. He was convinced of Robert Wilson's innocence only one night earlier.

"I think Moretti got orders from Captain Morales," whispered John. "They had a heated conversation just before your arrival. So, watch your back."

That should have worried me a little, but it didn't. We were close to the interrogation room when we saw Robert Wilson talking with a white-haired, elegantly dressed man. Two officers were watching him closely. Hearing our footsteps, the white-haired man turned to us, and a big smile appeared.

"Tony Moretti!" he exclaimed, looking in Moretti's direction. "You look a little different since I last saw you."

"You have also changed," said Moretti. "You got old. But I see you continue to choose the most difficult cases."

"Well … some priority clients … you know…" the man said arrogantly.

"Our evidence links your priority client to a murder," concluded Moretti.

"Ah, yes, of course," the white-haired man mockingly replied. "The infamous serial killer. Are you up to solving a case like this one?"

It was obvious they shared a common hatred.

"By the way, I'm Bradley Connor, Mr. Robert Wilson's lawyer," he said, addressing John and me. "And who is this young man and this magnificent lady?" he asked Moretti.

"Those are Detectives Liv Olsen and John Freeman. I assigned the case to them."

"Detective Liv Olsen! Oh! She looks to me more like a fashion model. I don't understand why she became a detective! Beautiful women like her love public adoration."

"They also love putting murderers in jail," I said.

"Oh, my! She is also quick-witted," he exclaimed. "I'm sorry to disappoint you, young lady, but Mr. Wilson is innocent. I have his alibi right here."

He put his hand in the inner pocket of his jacket, took out an envelope, and gave it to Moretti.

"So, we're done here?" asked Robert Wilson with a relaxed smile.

"Yes, Mr. Wilson, we are," said Bradley Connor. "We are leaving."

"Not before we check the alibi," I said.

Robert Wilson's eyes snapped to mine, and for a moment, his face had an icy look.

"Do you have to do this with me?" asked Bradley Connor, addressing Moretti.

"No. You can leave," was the answer.

I wanted to object, but Moretti made me shut up.

"I hope to see you more often," said Bradley Connor to Moretti. "And you," he said, turning to me, "you're too beautiful to stay in this nasty job."

I was tempted to put him off with some withering remark, but he was already walking toward the exit. Instead, I turned to Moretti.

"Excuse me, Sergeant, but what was that? Since when do we let an alleged murderer go without checking his alibi?"

"Save it, Olsen!" said Moretti. "I know what I'm doing. We don't stand a chance with Bradley Connor. He has all the judges, rich businessmen, politicians, and even the mayor in his pocket. He has never lost a case."

Something about his tone was like a slap on the face.

"This does not mean we should not check his alibi

before…"

He didn't let me finish my sentence.

"I'm sure Robert Wilson's alibi is rock solid. You will see for yourself. He is untouchable as long as Bradley Connor is his lawyer."

While I tried to shake off my irritation, our phones started ringing; we got another body. We looked at our phones and then at each other. We all knew that Miami is a dangerous place, being one of the most important cities for drug trafficking, but it seemed that lately, there had been a malignant force at work.

"Go," said Moretti.

I wasn't familiar with the part of Miami where we were going, but I thought John, a city native, might know it.

"I know this address," he said as if he'd guessed my thoughts. "It's in the Haitian neighbourhood. If I'm not mistaken, I think it's a church where they perform exorcism."

"How well do you know about Haitian beliefs?"

"What you mean is, do I have any special insight because I'm Black?"

"Do you?"

"I know they don't like detectives."

"That's all?"

"Is an insular culture. Haitian voodoo is based on West African voodoo. Some Haitians cultivate a personal relationship with their distant supreme creator by giving offerings, creating private altars and devotional objects, and participating in elaborate music, dance, and spiritual possession ceremonies. I may be Black, but I'm Cuban. Different culture."

"You live not far from their neighbourhood. You don't know anybody from their community?"

"I do. But the people I know don't mix with those worshiping the devil."

"It looks like they are also worshiping death."
"Yeah … among other things," mumbled John.

CHAPTER 23

The church was in the back of an alley. There were no parking spaces. John jammed the car onto the sidewalk, and we jumped out into the thinning crowd. We walked toward the place where uniformed cops kept a tight perimeter around the crime scene.

The body of a young woman was lying on the ground, the visible part of her face savagely damaged.

I scanned the body head to toe, wondering what monster could have done that. Within minutes, the entire team was on site. One of the cops had grabbed a middle-aged man by the shoulder and forced him in front of us.

"Damn, Mami! If I knew homicide detectives look like you, I would get arrested more often," said the middle-aged man, looking at me.

"Knock it off!" said the policeman.

"I found him at the corner of this building," he told us. "He's known for whipping out his johnson in mixed company. His name is Pierre Abraham. He's on parole for possession."

"Ah!" exclaimed John. "Did you whip it out in front of this young woman, Abraham?" he asked. "And when she wasn't impressed, you whipped out your knife instead?"

"Look, men! She's almost a kid! I prefer them with big tits and a nice ass. I saw her coming out of the church, but when I left, she was fine."

"I think you just put yourself at the crime scene. Cuff him," John said to the police officer.

"All right, I confess," said Abraham.

"You confess? To murder?" asked John.

"Hell no! To sparking up a blunt."

"So, you're getting baked while you're on parole?"

"Right outside the church. But when I lit up, I heard screaming."

"Who was screaming?"

"The chick. Oh, and I heard some dude, too."

"Did you see anything?"

"You gonna help me with my parole violation if I did?"

"Maybe," said John.

"All right. I saw some dude dragging the chick to a car."

"And you just kept smoking?"

"I thought she was his daughter, and she ran from home or something. You know what I mean."

"What did he look like?"

"I don't know. Uh … like a dude."

"White, Black, Asian?" I asked.

"Uh…"

"What about the car?" asked John.

"It was a car, man!"

"Like a sedan, an SUV, what?"

"Maybe an SUV … I don't know, man. By that time, I was wasted."

"John, I think we're wasting our time," I intervened. "Cuff him and take him to the station," I told the police officer.

"You said you would help me with my parole violation!" complained Abraham.

"We said maybe. Try to remember everything you have seen, and we are open for discussion."

We left Maria and Michael to check the neighbourhood, and John and I entered the church.

It was hot and humid inside, and there was no air conditioning. A suffocating cloud of sweet incense rolled over us, and we saw dozens of people dressed in long, colourful robes singing, shouting, and moving to the rhythm of several drums and the sound of bells.

"You are not allowed to enter the church during the ceremony," an old man stopped us.

"We want to talk to the church leader," said John, pointing to his badge.

The older man disappeared among the dancers and returned a few minutes later, accompanied by a giant guy with a low forehead, his face painted white.

"I'm the leader of this church," he said. "And who are you?"

We pulled out our badges and showed them to him.

"You must have the decency to wait until the ritual ends."

"There is a dead young woman outside the church, and we want to know if you, or anyone else here, knows her," said John.

"Everybody knows her; that's why I'm performing a ritual for expelling the demons."

"And how will your ritual help her?"

"We perform a purification ritual. We are fighting hard for the young woman's soul. The devil was strong in her. And the devil killed her."

"You see, Father, I don't think the devil killed her," I said.

"Yet, you should believe. You must be a Catholic. The Catholic church is doing exorcism, too."

"Good to know. But we need to find the human devil who killed her. Meaning we have to talk to every person in this church."

"Why?"

"We just want to ask if someone saw something."

"Nobody saw nothing."

"How do you know?" I asked.

"Because they would've told me."

"We will still have to question them."

"This is a house in mourning. It is time for you to go. The forces of evil are powerful."

"I can handle evil," I said.

"Not this kind, you can't."

He looked at me like he wanted to say "Don't try me."

"We will wait outside until you finish," I said. "Until then, no one should leave the church."

"You will need a warrant if you want to return inside."

"We will have one."

"You are wasting your time. All the people here are innocent."

"That is for us to decide," I said.

The leader took a step toward the door and opened it.

"As I said, you're wasting your time," he insisted. "And now, if you don't mind, you must leave the church."

"Something is going on here," John said as we stepped outside.

"I agree. The leader is determined to get rid of us."

"Let's call for a warrant right now."

The moment he pulled out his phone to call, his phone started to ring.

"It's Moretti," he said.

"See what he wants; I'll go talk to Philippe."

Around us, everybody was busy. Philippe and Tom worked slowly around the area where the girl had been found, trying to find some evidence. The sun was already shining brightly, and the heat became overwhelming.

"Hey, Philippe. What have you got?" I asked.

"Prints and DNA. There are a lot of smart criminals out there, but we still get the occasional moron. Like this one."

"Good work, Philippe."

Philippe was giving me one glance of triumph when I heard John's voice.

"Back door! Move!" he was shouting, already running for the corner of the church.

Several cops ran in the same direction. I heard a door slam and John's voice telling somebody to stop. A petulant voice was rising, and the church leader came into view, his hands cuffed behind him, followed by John, who had a black bag in his right hand.

"You have no reason to arrest me … you detective shit," shouted the church leader, addressing John. "God will punish you for arresting one of his disciples."

"God may be busy with religious matters when you will be found guilty," replied John.

"You will pay, you dirty cop, I will see to it."

However, the threats and the vocabulary used by the church leader made no apparent impression on John. He pushed him forward toward a police car.

"Get in the car, Father," he ordered.

The whole team had their eyes riveted on John, who was fast approaching.

"Can you explain what just happened?" asked Maria.

"Go on, open it," said John, throwing the black bag in front of her.

I leaned forward for a look. It was money. Lots of it. This explained the leader's reaction when we mentioned the warrant.

"Holy shit," exclaimed Maria. "That can't be coincidence. He's definitely involved in the girl's death."

"Wow! I'm impressed! When did you get so smart,

Sherlock?" John teased her.

"Ah! I've always been smart," said Maria. "Not that anyone would notice," she muttered more to herself.

"Well, you now have the chance to prove it," John said, smiling. "The case is yours and Michael's. Liv and I have to get back to the station. Moretti's got a lead on Miller's case."

By the time we returned to the station, it was already half past noon. We paced for a while, waiting for Moretti to leave the captain's office.

"I think we're on to something," Moretti said as soon as he stepped out. "As I told you earlier, I sent men to question the owners of the Toyota Highlanders that Wang had considered suspect. All had solid alibis except for one. His name is Logan Murphy."

"Have they arrested him?" asked John. "He was nowhere to be found. Our men, they are still looking."

"What about the car?" I asked.

"His car is nowhere to be found either. I put a BOLO on both."

"What do you want us to do?" I asked.

"Find out everything about Logan Murphy. Start with his family. I already got you a warrant."

CHAPTER 24

The address Moretti gave us was in an apartment building in a poor neighbourhood.

We went up to the third floor and rang the doorbell. A plain woman in her mid-forties opened the door.

"Mrs. Murphy?"

"Yes! And who are you?"

'I'm Detective Liv Olsen, and this is my partner, Detective John Freeman."

"Any news about my husband?"

"The police are doing everything to find him. Can we come inside? We want to ask you a few questions."

"Of course."

"When was the last time you saw your husband?" I asked.

"Three days ago. He came to have breakfast with our son."

"What do you mean he came? He doesn't live here?"

"No. After the foreclosure of our house, we separated. He rents a small apartment on the second floor. He wanted to keep a close relationship with our son."

I exchanged a look with John: Moretti hadn't given us

this information.

"Have you checked if he's in his apartment?" asked John.

"That was the first thing we did. My son has a key."

"Have you noticed a change in your ex-husband's behaviour lately?"

"Nothing that would have caught my attention. But I don't talk to Logan much. It's his fault that we live in this dump. I stay in my room while he has breakfast with our son."

"What does your ex-husband do for work?" I asked.

"He's an accountant."

"We need his work address."

She scribbled something on a piece of paper and handed it to me.

"Mrs. Logan, accountants get good salaries. Can you tell me how you got a foreclosure on your house?" I asked.

She seemed a bit annoyed with my question.

"Well, Logan was a compulsive gambler. I had no idea until we lost the house."

"Do you know if he owed anyone money?"

"Not that I know of. Why? You think his disappearance has something to do with an unpaid debt?"

"It's a pretty solid motive," I said.

She put a hand to her brow and sighed heavily.

"Oh, God! He promised our son he would never play again."

"Look, Mrs. Murphy, we're just trying to find a reason for your ex-husband's disappearance," I said.

"I just need to know what's happening, or I'll lose my mind thinking how it will affect my son."

"Is your son here?" asked John.

"He's in his room."

"Do you mind if we talk to him?"

"I'm afraid he's not going to be much help."

"You don't know that."

"All right."

She crossed the living room and knocked on the door on the left. The young man who opened the door looked at us warily.

"Billy, these are Detectives Olsen and Freeman," Mrs. Murphy said. "They would like to ask you some questions about your father."

"Aren't you supposed to be looking for him instead of being here?" asked Billy. "I read that if you don't find a missing person in the first 48 hours, the chances of finding them alive drop by 50%. Is that true?"

"Yeah, it's true," I said. But there is an even chance that he will be found."

"Was there anything unusual about your father's behaviour lately?" asked John.

Billy shook his head.

"No. He was his usual self."

"When you saw him last time, he didn't mention that he would be gone for a while?"

"No."

"Do you have any idea who would wish to harm your father?" I asked. "Even if it is just a feeling, a sense of unease about someone? Something that didn't sit right?"

"Like I said, he was his usual self."

"As painful as this is, I'm going to ask you to dig deep and think about any money issues your father may have been experiencing."

"I've done nothing but think, and there's nothing. Absolutely nothing."

"We would like to see your father's apartment. Mrs. Murphy told us you have a key."

"Do you have a warrant?"

"Yes, buddy! We do," said John, taking the warrant out of his pocket.

"Sorry," said Billy. "But I don't like people going through my father's stuff."

"We only want to find your father," said John.

"Right. Right," mumbled Billy.

We followed him to the second floor. The apartment was small and impersonal. An unpleasant smell came from the beige carpet that covered the floor. Next to the window was a shelf filled with books and a picture of Jeff with a man in his fifties.

"This is my father," Billy said, showing us the picture.

The man in the picture was shorter than his son, with a prominent belly hanging over his belt and a candid look.

"Does your father have a passport?" asked John.

"Of course! Why?"

"We'd just like to see it."

"I'll get it. I know exactly where he keeps it."

"Thank you."

We followed him into a room that appeared to be a bedroom and office. He was rummaging through a drawer.

"The passport is not where he usually keeps it," he said a few seconds later. "Maybe he put it somewhere else. Do you think he could have gone away?"

"It's possible," John said.

"Is this tablet your father's?" I asked him.

"Yes, it's my dad's old tablet."

"Do you mind if we take it? Might be useful."

"What do you mean?"

"There might be something on there to help us find your dad. We'll have it back by tomorrow."

"Sure. Anything that can help you find him."

"Thanks, Billy."

"I'll let you do your work," he said, walking quickly toward the exit, trying to hold back his tears. "You should bring me the key when you're done."

"Will do," I told him.

Reaching into my pocket, I pulled out a card.

"Give us a call if he contacts you."

He took the card and hurried out of the apartment.

I started checking the drawers in the bedroom when I heard John calling me from the living room.

"Liv, look at that: duct tape, a rope, hooks, and a scalpel."

"A kill kit," I said.

"Yeah … it looks like we found one of our killers."

"Don't touch anything. Call Philippe to come and take it to the forensics lab."

While John contacted Philippe, I continued to check the apartment.

"Did you find his passport?" asked John, who had finished his conversation with Philippe.

"No. If Logan Murphy is guilty, he probably left the city, maybe even the country."

"You know, when you look at Logan Murphy's picture, a little overweight guy with a candid look, it's hard to believe that he is mentally and physically capable of committing such heinous crimes!" said John. "But then, I remembered what you told me."

"And what was that?"

"You said that one of the most essential features of the psychopath is that he is strikingly sure of himself in situations where others would tremble with sweat and fear, which gives him a lot of power over his victim."

"Which is true. However, I thought the same as you when I looked at his picture. The only explanation would be that Logan Murphy is dominated by his partner, who must be a strong and violent man."

We continued to check the apartment until Philippe arrived with his new trainee and two police officers.

"Hi, you two," he said. "If you're done here, I need you

to leave so I can check the evidence."

We showed him what we found and left the apartment.

"What now?" asked John.

"We're going to Logan Murphy's workplace. Maybe we'll find something out from his colleagues."

"Shouldn't we report to Moretti first?"

"And waste time? Now that we have a lead, let's follow it."

"All right," he said. "Let's hope we arrive before closing time. It's almost five o'clock, and the traffic will be hell."

We rolled across town through light traffic, following the direction indicated on the GPS. Thirty-five minutes later, we pulled into a circular parking lot in front of a modern building. The number we were looking for was on the top floor. We went down to the end of the hall until the last door. A sign on the door that read *"Giving Hope - Children's Charity Organisation"* hung above the entrance.

I blinked. It couldn't be a coincidence.

"Isn't that the company Nancy Connery works for?" asked John.

"That's the one. She's the manager."

"I'll be damned! You may be right to be suspicious of her."

"Let's see what she has to say."

The door opened as we wanted to walk inside, and a young woman almost bumped into us.

"Sorry," she said. "I'm Deborah Lindsay, the secretary here at Giving Hope. How can I help you?"

"We're looking for Nancy Connery," I said.

"And you are?"

"I'm Detective Liv Olsen, and he's Detective John Freeman."

"Do you have identification? I'm sure you are who you say, but one can never be too careful these days."

We showed the young woman our badges.

"Thanks. Mrs. Connery has a charity event, and most employees are there to help her. I will be joining them soon."

"We need the address," John asked.

She took a pencil and paper from her purse and wrote the address.

"Thank you, Ms. Lindsay. We'll see you at the event."

CHAPTER 25

The traffic had gotten a little thicker than before, but most of it was going away from work in the city toward home in the suburbs. The lobby of the Hilton Hotel downtown, where the charity event was being held, was crowded with people: families and retired couples, businessmen, young women wearing minimal clothing flirting with young males, all happy to enjoy a pleasant evening after a perfect beach day.

I let myself be impregnated for a moment by the excitement floating in the air, wanting to forget that there is evil in the world, the kind that can turn a beautiful evening like this into a nightmare.

When we arrived at the event venue, the program had already started.

"And now I give the floor to our president, Mrs. Nancy Connery," announced a young man.

"Thank you, Brian," said the exquisite woman who approached the microphone.

"Hello, everybody! What a great turnout. A warm welcome to everybody present in support of children without a home.

Children touch everyone's hearts; they are our future, and I would like to thank the generous donors, the devoted staff, and the volunteers. You have tailored their care to meet their physical well-being and emotional, cultural, and educational needs."

Slowly, her speech became motivational, encouraging donors to feel good about their contributions and to dig even more deeply into their pockets.

"If she is a killer, we will need overwhelming evidence to prove it," said John.

"She is a good performer, isn't she?"

"The best. If I didn't know what I knew, Nancy Connery is a good person devoted to the well-being of orphans."

"Some psychopaths are good at hiding their natural predatory instincts. They are charming and very good at manipulating people. But they are always in search of a target."

"She just finished her speech; let's take the opportunity to talk to her before the donors approach her."

We walked over to where Nancy Connery stood.

"Mrs. Connery, I am Detective Liv Olsen, and this is my colleague, Detective John Freeman," I said, pulling out my badge. "We'd like to ask you a few questions, if you don't mind."

She lost her happy expression, and for a split second, there was a very unpleasant look on her face, which she replaced, without visible effort, with a relaxed smile.

"I'm sorry, Detectives!" she said, looking from my badge to my face, "As you see, I'm busy. Can you tell me what this is about?"

"This is about one of your employees, Mr. Logan Murphy."

"Excuse me for interrupting, Mrs. Connery," said the young man, Brian, appearing at our side. "The donors insist on talking to you."

"All right, Brian," she said. "I'll be there in a minute."

Then she turned to us and cleared her throat.

"I'm sorry, Detectives, but this event is significant for me and especially for children. What if I came to your headquarters tomorrow and we talked? Let's say, around eleven o'clock?"

"We appreciate your cooperation," John said, giving me one glance of surprise.

"Wonderful," Nancy Connery said, then she turned and walked toward a group of donors.

"That was a complete surprise," said John. "Usually, guilty people don't like to set foot in police stations!"

"Don't be so sure. People like her have the advantage of being incapable of feeling things, including guilt, and they have potent brains. I'll bet she'll be as comfortable in the interrogation room as she looked tonight at the event."

"You really think she's guilty?"

"I strongly feel she's somehow involved, don't you?"

"I'm not saying she's innocent, but I can't ever get my head around how a woman could do those horrible things to someone."

"Well, you must look at those kinds of women as victims themselves. They are typically very damaged people, ripe for abuse."

"And the abused become the abusers. Somebody like Nancy Connery."

"Exactly."

I could hear my phone ringing as I entered the parking lot; it was Jensen.

"Give me a minute," I told John.

"Hurry up! They may be waiting for us at the station," John said, waking toward the car.

I grabbed my phone, but the ringing had stopped. I scrolled down to Jensen's number and pressed the call button. A thrill coursed through my body as I waited for him to answer.

"Hi," he said. "I thought you didn't want to talk to me."

"Hi. Sorry, I was busy. Where are you?"

"I am on my way back home. I miss you," he whispered.

"I miss you too."

"I'll see you tonight?"

"Chances are I'll end up working very late."

"I don't care how late you finish. I want to see you. Promise me you'll come."

"All right. I promise."

I hung up and joined John in the car.

"I just talked to Moretti," John said. "They've got nothing on Logan Murphy. He has completely disappeared."

"People don't just disappear. They leave trails; forensic trails, paper trails…"

"Some of them are very good at disappearing."

"Yeah, well, they're not better than us."

"Not always. But this time, it looks like Logan Murphy got away. There is a team still looking for him. We have to hope he didn't run too far."

"I'm starving. Let's get something to eat on the way; it might be a long evening."

"We're almost at headquarters; we better order something. I'll make you try some real Cuban food."

"I love Maduros."

"Then Maduros it is," he said.

When we got to headquarters, the delivery man was already there with our food. Maria and Michael had just finished their report, and Moretti was already gone.

"What happened?" John asked Maria. "Did you get the church leader to talk?"

"We didn't need to make him talk. Thanks to Pierre Abraham, the guy who was on parole for possession, we were able to settle the case."

"Was it a drug operation?"

"It was. We arrested four men who were working with the leader. "

"Jesus Christ! What an asshole! How is it that Abraham knew about all this?"

"He has an addiction. He was buying the stuff from them."

"What about the girl?"

"The church leader and his men got her brother addicted, and the young woman threatened to expose them."

"And they killed her!"

"Apparently, they did not intend to kill her; they just wanted to scare her."

"Make sure they get the maximum sentence."

"We will."

"What about you? Have you got anything yet?" asked Michael.

We made them aware of Logan Murphy's disappearance and the facts that pointed to him as one of the two killers.

"That's excellent news!" exclaimed Michael. "I'm sure we will get the son of a bitch."

"It's a big world out there," John said. "If the team doesn't find him tonight, chances are he's left town."

"Look. We've done all we can for today," Michael said. Let's go home and relax our brains."

"We still need to write our reports."

"Right. See you tomorrow then."

CHAPTER 26

As I wrote my report, I had an unreasonable feeling that something was wrong with the facts that indicted Logan Murphy. It seemed too easy. Until now, we had had no clue who the killers were, and suddenly, we received overwhelming evidence on a silver platter.

I flipped through the report one last time and left, deciding not to think about it anymore. But the unshakable and unreasonable feeling stayed with me until I rang Jensen's doorbell.

"Hi," I said.

"Hi," he replied. We stood there staring at each other, the atmosphere charged between us. He grabbed me and pulled me to him.

"I missed you," he whispered.

"I missed you too."

His embrace became more insistent, and I forgot all the tension from the day.

Suddenly, he pushed away from me, leaving me breathless.

"Sorry," he said. "I got carried away by my feelings. I

should've asked you if you're hungry, or perhaps you want something to drink?"

I took a deep, steadying breath.

"I've already eaten. I need to shower," I said, my voice husky.

"Can I join you?"

"You may."

I undressed and slipped quickly into the shower. The water was warm and soothing, and I held my face to the welcoming torrent. Jensen undressed and joined me. He reached for a bottle of body wash and rubbed the soap onto my body, massaging firmly with his long, strong fingers.

"You are so beautiful!" he whispered.

My whole body clenched in anticipation, my senses disconnected, solely concentrating on what he was doing to me.

"Open your eyes," he whispered.

I opened my eyes, my blood pulsing hot and heavy. He was watching me, measuring my need, blue eyes darkening. His hands glided across my breasts, down to my belly and my hips, and the pressure built inside me.

"You like that?" he whispered in my ear.

"Hmm…"

My short, breathy reply was almost a gasp. His fingers were exploring my body, teasing, holding me so tight that I could feel the full force of his passion unleashed.

"Oh, baby, you feel so good," he murmured.

I felt the cool, smooth, tiled wall at my back, gasping at the invading, heavenly pleasure, spiking hot and harrowing from deep within me.

I peeked up at him through my lashes, and he was gazing at me with hooded eyes, his gaze burning, carnal, full of sensual longing.

"What do you want, Liv?" he breathed.

"You," I gasped.

His hands swept down my slick, wet body, and he showed no mercy, teasing and taunting, worshipping me.

"So beautiful," he murmured. "I will never get enough of you."

He continued the slow, delicious torture, his tongue against what felt like the most sensitive part of my body. I ran my hands into his hair and surrendered myself to his desire. My body tightened as he softly whispered my name, wrapped his arms around me, and found his release.

As the water spilled around us, I realized how empty my life would be without him.

"I never met anyone like you, Liv," he said, wrapping a towel around his waist and holding out a large towel to me. He stood very close, staring intently into my eyes, watching my reaction. I leaned up and kissed him. "Let's have a drink," he said, satisfied by my response.

He retrieved a bottle of wine from the fridge and two glasses from the kitchen cabinet. Then he signalled me to follow him outside.

For a few moments, we sat in silence, relaxing in the comfort of the sofa and enjoying the cold wine. Except for the lapping of the waves, the night was surprisingly calm.

"Did you catch Briana's killer?" asked Jensen, breaking the silence.

"No. Since then, we've had more victims."

"Who are the other victims?"

"I thought you knew about it; it's all over the news."

"I was busy twenty-four hours a day with this case in New York. Do you have any evidence or witnesses?"

"The only evidence we have is that there are two killers. We did have a witness, but she got killed because I didn't protect her."

"What do you mean by that?"

I told him about Gloria.

"You should not feel guilty about her death; it is your superior's fault. Guilt is a heavy burden to bear. One of my best friends, Steve, committed suicide because of guilt."

His eyes darkened as if the memory had disturbed his inner peace.

"How did that happen?" I asked him.

He hesitated momentarily, and when he began to speak, his mind seemed far away, memories flashing to his brain.

"We were a specialized unit, a tight-knit team of just six members. Our mission was to locate and apprehend a notorious leader of an infamous group for beheading western captains and orchestrating large-scale acts of terrorism. He was the driving force behind their extremist ideology, the head of the serpent. Considered our top public enemy, it was our duty to eliminate him."

He fell silent as if grappling with the memories of those moments. After a pause, he took a long sip of wine and continued.

"Steve was our sniper. He positioned himself in tall buildings, observing our every move and providing cover for us. He had to make split-second decisions, determining whether a suspect was preparing for a suicide attack or was innocent. It was an immense responsibility. You could be held accountable for a crime, but if you hesitated too long and the individual detonated himself, killing one of us, you would have to carry that decision for the rest of your life. In those moments, time seemed to slow down, freezing everything. Every decision made changes you. Sometimes, the struggle within is far greater than what we let on back home."

"Don't you usually have a suspect in mind?" I inquired.

"Only sometimes. In a war zone, anything goes. You never know who might appear wearing a suicide vest. It could be a woman or even a child, a martyr in the making."

"How do they convince them to embrace such a horrific death?"

"They brainwash them completely, convincing them that it's their duty, as per the teachings of the Quran, to kill all non-believers. Wearing the suicide vest and sacrificing themselves is their ultimate act of devotion to Allah."

"What happened to your friend?" I asked out of curiosity mixed with concern.

"That day, he made the wrong call. He hesitated to shoot a woman who was wearing a suicide vest, and it exploded. The blast threw me up against the wall, my ears ringing and blood dripping, but I survived. Crawling through the debris, I desperately searched for my team members. Two of them didn't make it."

"Is that why your friend took his own life?" I inquired sympathetically.

"I believe so. That day scarred him, and he couldn't shake off the memories. Back home, he succumbed to his inner demons. Only a select few know the truth of what transpired that day."

He fell silent, his gaze fixed on some distant point in the night. I could have shared my experience of witnessing a close friend's brutal death at the hands of a street gang, the feeling of helplessness as her fragile body succumbed to its injuries. But I decided enough ghosts were haunting us.

"Were you a sniper, too?" I asked, attempting to redirect the conversation.

He stared at me for a long moment as if grounding himself in the present.

"No," he finally responded. "I was always the better marksman, but Steve excelled as a spotter in sniping. I was the tracker."

"What does that entail?" I inquired, genuinely curious.

"It means you have to focus and locate your target. You

move forward methodically, with caution, relying on your senses of hearing, sight, smell, and touch. The entire team depends on you."

"Why tracking?" I probed further.

"Because I was the best at it," he replied.

"I suppose the special forces group you belonged to was a Navy SEAL unit?" I guessed.

"To be a part of that group, you need at least five years' experience as part of a SEAL team. But that's not something I can talk about."

He fell silent for a long moment, once again wrestling with the memories of those moments.

"You should know something about me," I said, breaking the silence. "I'm a very jealous person. I will not share you with anybody, including your demons. So, you have to chase them away."

"I'm sorry. Memories of war take you to some incredibly dark places. It can cost you your soul. For a long time, I felt nothing, no emotions, like everything was dead inside me. Until I met you."

He took the glass from my hand and put it on the table. He leaned down and touched me, unleashing sensations I had never felt so strongly.

CHAPTER 27

As I hurriedly grabbed a coffee the following day, the entire floor buzzed with preparations for a trip to a crime scene. I had little time to spare, anxiously waiting to learn the forensic findings regarding Logan Murphy. But there was no new information beyond what I already knew: that he was still missing and there was a BOLO on him.

Just as I managed to catch up with John, he swiftly turned the car around, and I climbed in. The sirens blared as we arrived at the south edge of the Little Havana area, where the crime had occurred, followed by Maria and Michael.
A small crowd had already gathered behind the yellow tape barrier erected by the police. All eyes immediately turned toward us, and the reporters eagerly began flashing their cameras, their questions pouring out.

"Detectives, can you share any information about the victim? Detectives…"

John snapped in exasperation, "They're like leeches, I swear."

Displaying our credentials, we crossed under the yellow tape, entering the crime scene. Maria, stepping into her role as team leader for the first time, wasted no time and approached one of the police officers, inquiring.

"What do we have here?"

With a sense of readiness, she was determined to face the challenges ahead.

"We have a floater in a jacuzzi," the police officer informed us.

The floater turned out to be a woman in her thirties. Someone had delivered a brutal blow to her head, shattering her skull. Blood pooled around the jacuzzi, accompanied by a multitude of identifiable footprints.

Kneeling beside the jacuzzi, I meticulously examined the bruises on her face and arms, evidence of her desperate attempt to shield herself from the assailant's relentless strikes. Dark traces beneath her fingernails indicated a struggle; the forensics team is better equipped to determine their nature than my naked eye could hope to ascertain.

"She has abrasions on her shoulders," Maria quickly pointed out. "Someone held her underwater."

Tom, who had just arrived, casually remarked, "At least she was having a good time before she died."

"You and your thoughtless comments," retorted Maria, clearly irritated.

"Why so glum, Maria? " said Tom, offering a glimmer of optimism. "Cheer up. Isn't this what you wanted to do? Be a detective?"

"Whatever," muttered Maria, rolling her eyes.

Taking charge, she rallied us all, eager to make her mark as the new team leader.

"Let's get to work," she said. "Liv, check the house for signs of a burglary. Michael and I will interview the neighbours, and John, you will search for surveillance cameras."

Inside the house, the scene mirrored its outward appearance; there was no evidence of a burglary or any attempt to stage the crime. Behind the back door, I found a lifeless dog. Its swollen body hinted at poisoning, a calculated move by the killer to eliminate any potential physical threat.

Coming out of the house, I saw John and Michael observing Maria as she presented Philippe with a blood-stained baseball bat. Catching sight of me, she enthusiastically beckoned, "Liv! We found the baseball bat used in the crime in a neighbour's trash can. Multiple fingerprints are present."

Her face was alight with a triumph as she shared her breakthrough.

"That's fantastic, Maria," I commended. "What do you think?" I asked Philippe.

"I still need to conduct lab tests, but I think we have his ass."

While Maria and Michael appeared to be deeply invested in the case, I was eager to return to headquarters.

"John and I must leave," I informed Maria. "We have an important witness to meet at eleven o'clock, and I can't afford to miss that meeting for anything."

"Is this regarding the Miller case?" she inquired.

"Yes, it is."

"Oh, my goodness! I almost forgot," John exclaimed. "Nancy Connery is coming at eleven. We need to get moving."

He glanced at his watch with a sense of urgency.

"We have to go now if we want to make it. I'll call Moretti and ask him to keep her occupied if we're running late."

"Good luck!" Maria exclaimed. "I hope you catch that son of a bitch."

The traffic was lighter, and we reached headquarters in approximately twenty-eight minutes. Sergeant Moretti was waiting for us at the front desk.

"Come to my office," he said, his mood unpleasant.

We followed him into his office, and I noticed my reports open on his desk.

"Fortunately," he began, "Mrs. Connery will be fifteen minutes late due to traffic, which will give me some time to clarify a few details. After reading your reports, Detective Olsen, it seems that Mrs. Connery is the suspect rather than a witness. Do you genuinely believe she could be responsible for these heinous crimes?"

"I can't accuse her without concrete evidence, but yes, I believe she may be involved somehow," I responded.

"We already have a viable suspect, Detective. We have evidence pointing to Logan Murphy as the culprit. And there is more. I'd asked Wang to check out any connections between Logan Murphy and the Miller family. After Murphy got foreclosed and evicted from his home, guess who bought his house?"

"Sunshine Build Group?" John guessed.

"That's right, Miller's company. I imagine Logan Murphy wasn't happy to walk away and lose all the money he already paid on the mortgage."

"I don't buy it," I said, risking a reprimand from Moretti.

"Why not?"

"It doesn't compute. These murders are complex, calculated, and personal. Why would somebody like Logan Murphy go to all that trouble just because Miller's company bought the house he had gambled away?"

"As we all know, gambling is a dangerous addiction," replied Moretti. "It can make you lose your mind. To exonerate himself of guilt, Logan Murphy blames Miller's company for the foreclosure of his house. I believe that was his reason to commit those crimes. Can't say the same about Nancy Connery."

"Well … all these horrible crimes are somehow connected to her."

"Do you understand what it means to accuse one of Miami's most influential individuals without overwhelming evidence? A person who has dedicated her life to helping orphaned children? Do you?”

“I do, Sergeant.”

A knock on the door interrupted our conversation, and a police officer entered.

“Excuse me, Sergeant, but a lady named Connery claims she has an appointment with Detectives Freeman and Olsen.”

“Escort her to the interrogation room and inform her they’ll be there shortly,” Moretti instructed.

“I hope I’ve made myself clear,” he added, looking directly at me. “Mrs. Connery must be treated as a witness and nothing more.”

“Understood, Sergeant.”

“Very well, then. Go and do your job.”

“What’s wrong?” John asked me as we were half the distance from the interrogation room. “You’re very quiet.”

“Well! It would help if you said something. You’re my partner.”

“Liv, Moretti is right for once.”

“What do you mean?”

“We have a viable suspect. All the evidence we have found proves that Logan Murphy is guilty. The connection with Nancy Connery may be just a coincidence.”

“That’s one hell of a coincidence.”

“Look, Liv. Nobody wants your gut to be right more than I do, but no matter how often we go over it, Logan Murphy is still guilty.”

“All right. Let us wait to see whether Philippe will come to the same conclusion after analyzing the evidence found in Logan Murphy’s apartment.”

CHAPTER 28

Moments later, I stood at the door of the interrogation room. I briefly paused to compose myself, then stepped inside, followed by John.

"Good morning, Mrs. Connery. Thank you for coming," I greeted her.

"Anything to assist with your investigation," she replied, offering a confident smile, albeit with a hint of artificiality.

John began the recording: "Nancy Connery 11:20 a.m.," he stated, indicating the date, time, and place, as well as our names as present detectives.

"Is this necessary?" asked Nancy Connery, pointing to the recording device.

"It is simply to document the information that you will provide us. It can be helpful to us later," I said.

"Very well. So, how can I assist you, Detectives?" she inquired.

"As we mentioned the other evening, this concerns one of your employees, Mr. Logan Murphy," I explained.

"Has something happened to him? He hasn't shown up for work in several days," she asked, expressing concern.

"That's precisely what we're trying to determine. Do you have any idea where Mr. Murphy might be?" I asked.

"Not really. I asked my secretary to contact him to see if he was ill, but she wasn't able to reach him. I've been preoccupied with organizing my charity event and didn't have time to consider his absence. But can you tell me what all this is about?" she questioned.

"How long has Mr. Logan been working for you?" I asked, evading her question.

"For about a year now," she replied.

"Did he usually miss work for several days at a time?"

"No, never. Logan wanted to prove to me that he deserved my trust," she explained.

"What do you mean by that?" I probed.

"Well, Logan had been a compulsive gambler for a few years. As a result, he lost his home and had trouble holding a job for long. When he came to me for the accounting assistant position, he was at the point of desperation," she revealed.

"And you hired him as an accountant, knowing he is a compulsive gambler?" I asked, seeking clarification.

"Accounting assistant. He didn't handle the money. He was eager to quit gambling and try to rebuild his life. Something about him convinced me he was telling the truth. And I was right. He did an excellent job. But you still haven't told me what all this is about," she pressed.

"Mr. Murphy is missing, and we hope you can provide us with any idea where he might be," I explained.

"The only thing I can think of is that he has returned to his bad habits and is spending all his time at the casino," she suggested.

"We have already checked, and he is not there," I informed her.

"Then I'm not sure I have anything else to tell you," she responded. "Logan and I have a strictly working relationship," she stated.

"Did he have a closer relationship with any of your employees?" I asked.

"Not that I know of," she replied.

"Have you noticed any changes in his behaviour recently?" I questioned.

"That's something you'll have to ask my secretary. Most of the time, I'm not in the office. I'm around town looking for donors," she explained.

"Mrs. Connery, did Mr. Murphy show aggression toward you or your employees?" I asked cautiously.

"No! Why? Did he assault anyone?" she inquired.

"He did."

Her eyes widened, and she took a moment to compose herself before responding.

"In that case, I hope you find him quickly. We have enough aggression in this city. And we expect the police to do something to stop it."

"We do everything we can."

"You are not doing enough. For example: do you have a suspect in the Miller family case?"

And there it was. As soon as I heard her question, I realized her true motive for offering to come to the station: to extract information about the Miller family's case. I decided to take a calculated risk and try to catch Nancy Connery in her own game.

"The horrible crimes committed against the Miller family should have opened old wounds for you," I stated, watching her reaction closely.

A flicker of surprise crossed her face.

"I'm not sure I follow," she responded, trying to maintain composure.

"We have reason to believe that there is a connection between the recent murders of the Miller family members and that of your husband twenty years ago," I revealed, intensifying my scrutiny.

Her confident facade wavered for a split second, and I saw a glimmer of unease in her eyes.

"I … I don't see how that could be possible," she said. "The police never solved the case and didn't apprehend my husband's killer."

"We've been investigating these cases diligently, and we've uncovered new leads that suggest a possible connection," I pressed, carefully observing her reaction. "We believe you may have valuable information to help us solve the Miller family case and your husband's murder."

She looked at me without expression, the complete absence of emotion unsettling.

"I … I don't remember much. It was a long time ago. My husband was dead, and everything was in pieces. I was shattered."

"It's okay. I understand that. I was just hoping you might remember things that can help us find the killers and bring justice to their families."

"Are you married, Detective?

"No, I'm not."

"Then you don't know what it means to find the right man, follow your heart, and then see your husband hanging from a rope. That single moment tore my world apart. It took me all those years to move on with my life. And now you want me to relive that nightmare?"

I had to admit she was a fantastic actress.

"I apologize, Mrs. Connery. Please take a moment to compose yourself. If you have no further information to provide, you are free to leave," I stated calmly, maintaining a professional demeanour.

Ceasing my questioning of Nancy Connery was imperative, as continuing to do so would jeopardize my position on the case, possibly leading to my removal by Moretti.

"Yes, I am distraught and would like to leave," she replied.

"Of course. Allow me to escort you outside," I offered, guiding her toward the exit door.

As we approached the door, she turned toward me, her expression filled with concern.

"Are you the lead investigator in the Miller case?" she inquired.

"Yes, that is correct," I confirmed.

"You must exercise utmost caution. These criminals pose a significant threat. It would be tragic if someone as beautiful as you were to meet the same fate as the other victims," she warned.

"I am resolute in my determination to apprehend the culprits," I assured her.

"In that case, you must be prepared for the consequences," she responded ominously.

Her eyes were holding a chilling darkness, drawing me in like a moth to a flame. Within that darkness resided a sadistic psychopath who revelled in the torment and suffering of others.

"You appear quite confident in your statement," I noted.

She gazed at me bleakly, her hand resting on the doorknob.

"I am merely offering you advice. Whether you choose to heed it is up to you," she replied.

With a shake of her head, she opened the door and departed. I stood there momentarily, realizing that she had indirectly threatened me, and a shiver ran down my spine.

The pursuit had taken a personal turn, evolving into a battle between my unwavering determination and the sadistic psychopath's insatiable appetite for cruelty.

CHAPTER 29

For a few minutes, I stood there, caught in the turmoil of whether to divulge the recent developments to Moretti. The mounting evidence against Logan Murphy demanded more than mere intuition to sway him. As I grappled with my decision, the shrill ring of my phone pierced the air, abruptly interrupting my thoughts.

"Olsen," I answered.

"Hey, Liv, it's Philippe. I have some answers for you," came his voice on the other end.

"I'll be right there," I responded, my curiosity piqued.

Making my way to Philippe's laboratory, I found him restlessly pacing in front of his desk. Spread across it were the tapes and ropes unearthed from Logan Murphy's apartment, the tangible evidence we had been waiting for.

"What have you discovered?" I inquired, unable to contain my anticipation.

"Well, after conducting a thorough investigation, it turns out that the lab technicians correctly identified the tapes and ropes as the ones used in the Millers' murders, and the fingerprints do match those of Logan Murphy," Philippe began, his tone carrying a mix of certainty and intrigue.

"That sounds quite conclusive," I remarked, though a flicker of doubt lingered beneath the surface.

"It does, Liv. However, here's where things get interesting. These tapes and ropes were supposed to … forgive me for getting a bit technical, but how well-versed are you in forensic matters?" Philippe asked.

"I have a decent understanding," I replied, urging him to continue. "Please get to the point."

"Fair enough. So, I consulted with the submission team at the laboratory to conduct a basic environmental analysis of these items. The team wanted to check whether the objects found in Logan Murphy's apartment showed distinct patterns of carpet fibre deposits," Philippe explained, his words hinting at a revelation yet to come.

"I see. As individuals move about a room, fibres become airborne and settle on nearby objects, providing insight into how long those objects have been in that particular location," I recalled, my mind racing to piece together the significance of his findings.

"Exactly. Surprisingly, none of the items associated with the crime scene showed any signs of carpet fibre deposits. Now, this raises concerns … you know what I'm getting at," Philippe expressed with a furrowed brow, his worry mirroring my own.

"Somebody might have planted these items," I acknowledged, the weight of the revelation sinking in.

"Exactly."

"Have you checked the footprints?" I inquired, hoping for a breakthrough.

"I did. All the footprints in the house match those of the resident, the officers, Murphy's son, you, and John. However, one imprint perfectly fits the one discovered at the crime scenes. This suggests someone else was in that apartment, and Logan Murphy may be innocent. He could also be another victim," Philippe concluded, his voice tinged with a mix of urgency and concern.

"That's precisely what worries me," I concurred, a sense of unease settling.

"If Logan Murphy was guilty and wanted to disappear, why would he leave such incriminating evidence against himself, knowing that his family would notify the police of his disappearance?"

"I agree. Unless something unexpected happened, and Logan Murphy had no other choice," Philippe speculated, his eyes searching mine for insight.

"I believe the real criminals have handed us a culprit on a silver platter, thinking we'll stop investigating. Which means they have a shallow opinion of our ability to analyze. Have you briefed Moretti?" I asked, my thoughts already racing ahead.

"No, I wanted to fill you in first. Moretti's going to freak out," Philippe responded, the weight of the impending storm evident in his voice.

"I know. Moretti will once again be under immense pressure from the media and the public," I added.

"Well, he'll have no choice but to accept reality. Evidence never lies," Philippe stated with a hint of determination.

"You're the expert on that," I acknowledged.

I reached for my cellphone, which had started ringing, and answered the call. It was John on the other end.

"They found Logan Murphy," he announced.

"Where?" I asked.

"In the Glades."

"Alive?"

"Dead. We have a suspect vehicle," John replied.

"What do you mean by that?"

"Someone was close by when the killer took the body

out of the trunk."

As I spoke, I started walking down the main hall, surrounded by the bustling activity of our team. Everyone seemed poised, waiting for Moretti's orders.

"Give me the air units right now!" Moretti's voice boomed, filled with urgency and authority. "I need birds in the air, people!"

The pilot's voice crackled over the radio, responding to Moretti's command.

"Unit four, over."

Moretti provided the pilot with the model and colour of the suspected car. The description matched that of Logan Murphy's car, which had disappeared along with its owner.

"Sorry, Sergeant," said John, who had thought the same as I did. "If Logan Murphy is dead, he's not one of the psychopaths we seek."

"This is what I want you and Detective Olsen to find out," replied Moretti, who seemed disappointed by the turn of events. Once again, he found himself at an impasse with the case.

Moments later, we heard the pilot's voice again.

"Unit four, I have a visual of the car on US-1, over," the pilot reported.

"Stay on him," Moretti commanded. "I'm ordering a roadblock."

"Will do, over," the pilot acknowledged.

"Okay, people. Go to the crime scene and turn over every rock," Moretti declared, addressing our team with a resolute tone. I wasn't surprised that he chose not to accompany us. He wanted to avoid the imminent storm of media scrutiny.

"Time to roll," said John, heading to the parking lot. "I'll drive."

Sirens wailed as we raced to the crime scene, followed closely by blaring ambulances. The investigation had taken an unexpected turn, and we grappled with a complex puzzle.

As our vehicle penetrated the mystical realm of the Everglades, I found myself captivated by the harmonious clash of nature's allure and its insatiable hunger for survival. This vast wilderness, adorned with lethal flora and fauna, held a paradoxical beauty that seduced and warned visitors. Alligators, crocodiles, manatees, and a myriad of vibrant bird species thrived within its borders, enticing adventurers with hiking trails, biking routes, and serene waterways for kayaking and boating.

Approaching the crime scene, we encountered only a handful of onlookers, their curiosity restrained by the barricade tape erected by the vigilant police.

We showed our credentials to the officers, and Philippe, Tom, and Gary set to work.

The on-site officers exuded an air of heightened alertness, a testament to their unwavering dedication to preserving the scene's integrity. It was clear that they understood the gravity of the situation and the necessity of shielding bystanders from the horrifying spectacle before us.

My gaze fell upon the victim, Logan Murphy, his body bound and his face a mask of unbearable pain. The meticulousness of the wounds left no doubt; they bore the unmistakable signature of the same ruthless killers who had preyed upon the Miller family.

No traces of blood stained the immediate surroundings, indicating that this site was merely a cold, calculated dumping ground for the lifeless shell before us.

I approached the officer who had scrutinized my credentials earlier, seeking details surrounding the discovery of Logan Murphy's body.

"The park security guards alerted us to a heated altercation between two groups of young individuals," the officer explained, his tone betraying a genuine concern for public safety.

"We're the nearest police station, and they sometimes call us if there are incidents they can't deal with," he explained. "We put on the sirens, and when we got close to this location, we saw someone running toward his vehicle and starting it with a bang. We got ready to start the chase, and that's when we saw the victim's body on the ground. I believe the criminal intended to throw the body into the water, poised to vanish within the unforgiving jaws of the Everglades' predators."

"And that's when you contacted dispatch," I interjected, seeking clarity.

"No," he replied. "We prioritized securing the crime scene, ensuring its integrity, and then coordinated with our colleagues to divert traffic away from this macabre sight, shielding the public from this horror."

Only then, after securing the scene and safeguarding its sanctity, did the officers reach out to dispatch with detailed descriptions of the culprit's vehicle: model, colour, and license plate number.

Silent skepticism swept through my mind. Had the officer's meticulousness inadvertently granted our killer precious time to disappear?

"Perhaps I should have called dispatch first," the officer said with a hint of regret.

Good. He was an intelligent cop but didn't have much experience.

"We all learn from our mistakes," I offered, masking my concerns with a reassuring tone.

The press abruptly moved in at that precise moment, shattering the tense atmosphere.

"Here they come," remarked John, who silently absorbed the cop's words. "How the hell did they find out so quickly?"

He walked toward the corner, where Philippe and Tom were diligently scouring for evidence, and I followed suit.

"Bingo!" exclaimed Tom as we drew nearer.

"What did you find, Tom?" I inquired.

"Take a look," he replied, gesturing toward a smudge of what appeared to be fresh blood on Logan Murphy's body. "Fresh blood. It could be the killer's blood. We might be able to get a DNA match."

"Even better," chimed in Philippe, pointing to a spot on the duct tape securing Logan Murphy's hands. "We also have a fingerprint here."

"Finally," I breathed out.

We were all excited as we eagerly awaited to check the results. Twenty minutes later, the medical examiner, Gary, finished examining Logan Murphy's body.

"This guy is dead for at least thirty hours," he declared.

"That means Sunday before noon," assured John.

"Exactly," confirmed Gary.

"There's no doubt that the killer is one of those who murdered the Miller family, Briana Cooper, and Gloria Perez," said John. "Do you agree with me?"

"It looks like it, but I can confirm it after more analysis," replied a cautious Gary.

Our work was done for the moment, and we couldn't wait for the fingerprints and DNA results.

CHAPTER 30

We drove back to US-1, where the traffic was thick enough to make me wonder whether we would get back to headquarters before nightfall. Miami was like a magnet for vacationers, and the promise of its sun-kissed beaches and vibrant nightlife drew people from all over.

With lights flashing and sirens blaring, we pushed our vehicles to the limit, seeking to escape the confines of the heavy traffic that threatened to slow us down. The ambulance that was carrying Logan Murphy's body did bravely keep up with us.

Then, a glimmer of hope came through the radio; our fellow officers apprehended the suspect's car, but the chase was far from over. We needed to find the driver who had escaped into a bustling shopping mall.

Arriving at the scene, the chaos was palpable. Police vehicles lined the area, and a crowd had gathered, curious to see what was happening. The yellow tape cordoned off the abandoned Toyota Highlander, silently witnessing the pursuit that had led us here.

The officer on the scene informed us that the driver had

vanished without a trace, leaving us without any description to aid our search. But then, ever observant, Tom noticed something crucial: the car seat was set unusually far back.

"Hold up a second," he said. "The car seat is set back like mine is. Farther, even."

"All right," said John. "So, we must be looking for a big guy."

"Oh! I think the word you are looking for is tall," Tom replied. "About six feet, at least."

This led us to the realization that we were likely dealing with a tall suspect, a detail that could significantly narrow down our search. The officer closest to me acted quickly, passing on the new information to the rest of the team.

Leaving Tom and Philippe to inspect the car, we set out to find the elusive suspect, knowing that time was against us. We split into teams inside the mall, combing through the busy shops and crowd.

As we scoured the shopping mall, our optimism started to wane. There were dozens of men in the mall who were six feet tall, and the suspect remained elusive, like a ghost in the crowd. We questioned shop owners and asked passersby if they had seen anyone who seemed suspicious. But it seemed like he had vanished into thin air.

Frustration began to set in, and the fading daylight only added to our sense of urgency. With each passing minute, the possibility of catching the suspect before nightfall grew slimmer. Still, we refused to give up.

As we regrouped near the mall entrance, I suggested reviewing the mall's security camera footage to see if we could spot the suspect's movements before he disappeared.

Quickly, we contacted the mall's security team, who agreed to cooperate with us. We gathered in the mall's security office, and a technician started combing through hours of footage from various surveillance cameras. Time passed slowly as we watched the screen, hoping for a breakthrough.

Finally, a grainy image caught our attention. The footage showed a tall man walking toward the mall's rear exit, looking furtively around him to see if anyone was following. There he was, the suspect we had been searching for.

We rushed back to our vehicles and sped toward the exit he was heading for. As we arrived at the mall's rear, the sun had dipped below the horizon, casting long shadows across the pavement. We cautiously fanned out, covering every possible escape route. It was a race against time and darkness.

Just as the night began to envelop us, we spotted a figure darting between parked cars.

"Stop! Police!" we shouted in unison.

The suspect hesitated momentarily, glancing back at us, and then attempted to make a break for it. But we were expecting that reaction, and with precise coordination, we closed in on him, blocking his path from every direction.

Realizing there was no way out, the suspect raised his hands in surrender, panting heavily from the adrenaline-fueled escape attempt. We had finally caught him. We checked his pockets and took out his identification papers. His name was Barry Lewis.

"Barry Lewis, you're under arrest for the murders of Harry Miller, Briana Cooper…" began John.

"What? I didn't kill anyone, man," exclaimed Lewis. "I only stole some electronics."

"Is that Toyota Highlander over there your vehicle?" asked John.

"No, man! I can't afford a car like that. My car's right over there," he said, pointing to an old Chevrolet.

"And didn't you drive that Toyota into the Everglades today?"

"I don't know what you're talking about, man. All

afternoon, I was in the mall and stole seven mobile phones and other electronics. You can find them in my car."

John was as confused as I was when we found the seven mobile phones, four laptops, and two digital cameras in Barry Lewis' car. We returned to the mall's security room, and the footage from the surveillance cameras confirmed that he had been there from noon onward. Barry wasn't the criminal we were looking for, but he was a criminal nonetheless. We decided to take him with us and transfer him to the appropriate department.

As I approached Tom and Philippe, my heart was pounding with anticipation, hoping they might have some breakthroughs in the case.

"What have you got for me?" I inquired, eager for any positive news they could share.

"Many things," replied Philippe.

I felt a surge of relief.

"If that means good news, I could use some right now."

"Well, we've got fingerprints, blood, hair, skin, and a scalpel," Philippe revealed.

"Awesome," I breathed, feeling the puzzle pieces starting to come together.

"Are you done processing everything here?"

"We are," Tom chimed in.

"Great. Then we should head back to headquarters," I suggested.

Back at headquarters, we accompanied Philippe and Tom to the lab, watching closely as they hurriedly logged in the samples they had collected from the crime scene and the car.

While the Fingerprint Identification System tirelessly searched its database, I took a moment to update Moretti on what had transpired in the Everglades and at the mall.

"Did you get any results from the lab?" inquired John,

who had stayed behind to handle the suspect.

"Not yet, no," I replied. "What about Barry Lewis?"

"He's quite the troubled individual. A history of petty crimes, occasional employment, but always reverting to stealing. He also has a violent past and spent nearly a decade in prison," John shared with a hint of disdain in his voice.

I wanted to say something about giving people a chance at redemption when our conversation was cut short as the Fingerprint Identification System made a match. Our attention was immediately drawn to the screen, where we saw a familiar face.

"Oh, my god! He looks just like Robert Wilson," Philippe exclaimed in astonishment. "But, according to the ID system, this guy's name is Lucas Mason," he added.

"And check this out," John said. "He's a surgical assistant at Miami Central Hospital. This guy knows how to handle a scalpel."

"This guy is not Robert Wilson," I declared confidently. "According to Gary, Logan Murphy was killed Sunday morning while Robert Wilson was already in our custody. He likely has an identical twin brother."

"I agree with Liv," Tom interjected, having approached silently. "I've just received the results from the DNA analysis, and you won't believe what we found."

Eager to get more answers, we followed Tom into his lab, where the system's screen displayed two identical photos of Robert Wilson and Lucas Mason, confirming that they indeed shared similar DNA.

For a long time, neither of us spoke. It was one of those moments when the questions were hanging in the air, and only the database could give us more answers.

"Here's the thing," Tom finally explained. "You have different fingerprints, but identical twins share the same DNA. Identical twins can be misidentified for a long time, especially in DNA analysis. They played us."

"We've got to arrest them both," John urged, ready to take immediate action.

"I have no reason to arrest Robert Wilson," declared Moretti. "I need more evidence before making a move. I can bring him in for questioning, but I lack concrete evidence against him. However, I'll send you with a team to Lucas Mason's house immediately, even though I doubt he's there after everything that's happened. I'll immediately put out a BOLO alert for him. You'll have to leave now, and I'll join you with the warrant. Go."

With the adrenaline rushing through my veins, I nodded, ready to pursue this new lead and hopefully uncover the truth behind the murders committed.

CHAPTER 31

The evening passed by in a blur of frantic activity. We reached Lucas Mason's opulent residence in Key Biscayne and quietly waited in the car until Moretti arrived. The neighbourhood was adorned with exquisite mansions, a haven for the wealthy who lived in utmost comfort and luxury and earned far more than a surgeon's assistant like Lucas Mason.

"Something is bothering me," said John. "I wonder if Lucas Mason can afford to live on an assistant's salary in such an expensive house," John pondered.

"I wondered the same thing when I saw the house and the neighbourhood."

"Perhaps he inherited the money."

"Perhaps. That's something we'll have to check out," I said. "Follow the money."

After his arrival, Moretti ensured that all potential escape routes from the house were covered, and John and I followed SWAT team members, ready to breach the door if necessary.

As expected, there was no response after ringing the bell, knocking, and announcing our presence. The SWAT team forcefully broke the door, and we stormed into the house, our guns ready.

To our dismay, there was no sign of Lucas Mason or anyone else inside. We started searching for any evidence that could implicate him. We meticulously combed through his drawers and examined his closets, discovering a vast collection of expensive clothing and shoes.

Upon entering his bedroom, I looked around, unsure what to search for. It was evident that Lucas Mason wouldn't make it easy for us to find evidence of his crimes, not even within his own home. But I was hoping to find something. Many psychopathic killers tend to keep trophies from their victims.

"Find anything of interest?" Moretti inquired.

"Not yet," I replied.

"What exactly are we looking for?" John asked.

"Anything that might be relevant," I stated.

"What could be more relevant than his DNA and fingerprints?"

"This man is exceptionally cunning," I said. "If we catch him, he might claim that Logan Murphy attacked him, forcing him to defend himself, resulting in accidental death. He could justify his escape as fear for his life."

"He's still a killer!"

"I agree. However, our evidence points to Logan Murphy as the serial killer, not him. And Lucas Mason knows this because he planted that evidence. With a skilled lawyer, he could get away with it."

"She's right," confirmed Moretti. "We need more proof. We have to…"

Our phones began ringing simultaneously: a cop had identified Lucas Mason in a bar on Ocean Drive and asked for help.

"Let's go," ordered Moretti. "The team will stay and search

the whole house."

We followed his car as he drove fast, weaving in and out of traffic at an excessive speed, even for police officers.

In the evening, Ocean Drive was the place to be, and Florida's most famous avenue was bustling with people as the nightlife was picking up.

Music wafted in and out of the car's windows, groups of girls giggled and flirted with guys, people of all ages lined up at nightclub entrances, and a festive atmosphere filled the air. It was the perfect setting for Lucas Mason to blend in and disappear without a trace.

Then, the traffic stopped, delaying our arrival at the bar where the cop had spotted Lucas Mason. We were just hoping he would still be inside.

Finally, we reached the address, and as we stepped out of the cars, Moretti gave clear instructions to the cop who identified Lucas Mason. The cop nodded, his eyes focused on the entrance, ready to pounce if Mason tried to escape.

We cautiously entered the lively bar, scanning the faces in the dimly lit room. Lucas Mason, or perhaps Robert Wilson, was sitting on a sofa, looking comfortable, glass in hand. Next to him sat a dark-haired woman in an exquisite dress, engrossed in conversation.

The three of us exchanged glances, pondering the same question: how could we tell which identical twin was sitting before us?

Our answer came as we approached him.

"Detectives! Are you here to celebrate something?" he asked, recognizing us right away, meaning he was Robert Wilson. In his seemingly confident smile, I noticed a fleeting flicker of panic.

"Darling, these are the detectives who mistakenly arrested me for the crime committed against that woman, Briana Cooper; I think that was her name," he said, addressing the woman beside him.

"I don't want to spoil your evening," said Moretti, "but we urgently need to ask you a few questions. Would you mind following us to headquarters?"

The dark-haired woman quickly interjected, trying to protect Robert Wilson from Moretti's inquiry.

"That's out of the question," she said defiantly. "We're celebrating our anniversary, and I won't let anything spoil our evening. Unless you have a warrant."

"You got your answer, Detectives," said Robert Wilson. "Ah! Sorry," he added. "She's my fiancée, Susan Richard. And as you know, she's a lawyer."

"As I said, we have questions, and only you have the answers," insisted Moretti, his patience wearing thin.

At Moretti's insistence, Wilson finally relented, agreeing to meet us at the police station at eleven-thirty the following day. But as we walked away, I couldn't shake the feeling that he was hiding crucial information and had no intention to give it to us.

"Did you find him?" asked the cop who had stayed behind to guard the bar's exit.

"No," replied Moretti. "But you did a good job anyway; keep up the excellent work."

"Ay, ay, Sergeant," replied the proud cop.

Back in our cars, Moretti expressed his concern over the case's complexity. Identical twins posed a unique challenge, and we had to investigate meticulously.

"If you don't mind me saying so, Sergeant," I spoke up tentatively, "there's also the possibility that Wilson is his brother's partner in crime and is exposing himself publicly to see how fast the police and the people will react. They look so alike that nobody can differentiate them. And now he likely knows we put a BOLO on his brother."

The suggestion took Moretti aback, but after a moment

of contemplation, he acknowledged my theory's validity.

"If, at first, I thought you were paranoid, I'm beginning to think you might be right, Detective Olsen. That's why, from now on, I want you and Detective Freeman to forget about other cases and give this case your full attention. And I'll provide all the help you need. I'll ask Wang to stay the night and dig deep into the twins' lives. Tomorrow morning, you'll have his report."

"Thank you, Sergeant," I said, wanting to add that he should have done it from the start, knowing that the stakes were high and lives were at risk.

"I think he's had enough of this case and is desperate to settle it," John said as he drove me to headquarters to pick up my car. "It's good that we can concentrate only on solving it instead of getting involved in many other cases."

"Well, it's about time. You must give a hundred percent to settle a case like this," I concluded.

John's stomach made a loud noise, and we both laughed. We hadn't eaten anything all day, and our stomachs were rebelling. I was also starving and badly needed a shower.

Exhausted and hungry, we parted ways for the night. I called Jensen to explain my delay and found comfort in the familiarity of his voice.

"I thought you'd never call," he said. "Long day?"

Hearing his voice made me realize how much I had missed him, even if it had only been a day since I'd seen him.

"Very," I replied. "And I'm starving."

"I'll order something right away. What do you want to eat?"

"Anything. I haven't eaten all day."

"How long before you arrive?"

"One hour. I have to go home first to get a change of clothes."

"You should bring more stuff here."

I disconnected the call without answering, not wanting to agree with him too quickly. My body hummed at the memory of last night, and my muscles contracted deliciously in my belly at the anticipation of what was to come.

CHAPTER 32

Arriving at work the following day, I found John sulking at his desk with coffee. The door opened before I could say something, and Lee Wang, the crime analyst, came in. He held up some paperwork.

"Got some results for you," he said, putting the file on the desk.

"I can see you didn't get much rest last night," I commented, observing Lee's tired appearance.

"I didn't. This case grows more complex by the minute. I'm glad it's not my job to figure it out."

Looking through the file, John asked, "Did you find out why the twins have different family names?"

"Read the report," Lee grumbled slightly as he walked toward the door. "If you have any questions, you know where to find me."

"He's not in his best mood today," John remarked.

"I can imagine. He must have spent most of the night compiling this report," I said, sympathizing with Lee's exhaustion.

"Let's dive into it; I'll make you a copy," John suggested,

eager to see what Lee had found.

The report revealed that the Wilson family adopted the twins from an orphanage when they were two. Their first names were Robert and Richard, not Robert and Lucas. Mr. Wilson, a doctor, and his nurse wife gave them a privileged education in private schools. The family later moved to Jacksonville, possibly closer to their extended relatives.

Robert attended the New York University School of Law, prompting the family's return to New York to allow him to study at the top-ranked law school in the United States. On the other hand, Richard faced challenges and ended up being accepted into the New York University College of Nursing after failing to secure a place in medical school.

"I wonder why Richard changed his name to Lucas? wondered John.

"We should continue reading; Lee might have the answer in the report. What's bothering me is the connection with Nancy Connery," I said.

"I don't see the connection!" said a surprised John.

"She left New York for Jacksonville and then back to New York almost simultaneously to the Wilsons."

"Right, she seemed to follow the Wilsons' moves. That can't be a coincidence," John agreed.

"Exactly. It feels like a crucial clue, but let's avoid jumping to conclusions. Let's see what else Lee has uncovered," I suggested, trying to stay focused.

We delved deeper into the report, hoping to find vital information to crack the case. Lee's detailed and accessible writing style made the investigation more manageable.

According to his research, Robert became a lawyer, while Richard worked as a surgical assistant. The report turned dark when it revealed that Richard's girlfriend was found murdered, with the murder weapon being a scalpel.

Although he had an alibi, Richard was still considered

the primary suspect. But the investigation was halted when Richard and his parents were pronounced dead in a severe car accident, with their bodies consumed mainly by the fire. A few months later, Robert Wilson moved to Miami and began working as a lawyer for Sunshine Build Group.

Lee ended his report by explaining that Richard Wilson hadn't just changed his name; he'd murdered Lucas Mason in order to impersonate him and join his brother in Miami. His theory was this: Lucas Mason was accepted into the New York University College of Nursing at the same time as Richard Wilson. After the final exam, he landed a job as a surgical assistant in New Jersey.

While working in New Jersey, he took a vacation in Florida, fell in love with a woman, and decided to move to Miami. A few months later, he got accepted as a surgical assistant at Miami Central Hospital. In Lee's opinion, there was only one explanation: Richard Wilson had presented himself as Lucas Mason to fill the surgical assistant position at Miami Central Hospital. The same day he moved to Miami, Lucas Mason's future wife conveniently committed suicide by poisoning herself.

Lee had yet to find further information on Lucas Mason.

"Considering all this, it's evident to me," John remarked, "that Richard Wilson killed Lucas Mason to impersonate him and follow his brother to Miami. There is no other explanation. What do you think?"

Before I could respond, Moretti joined us and tossed another copy of Lee's report on the desk.

"Have you finished reading Wang's report?" he asked.

"Yes, we have," John replied. "The information is overwhelming."

"I agree," I said. "I believe we now have enough to build a solid case."

"I'd like your conclusions," said Moretti.

"Richard Wilson, also known as Lucas Mason, is undoubtedly the culprit," I stated. "He likely killed his girlfriend and faked his death to avoid justice. The car accident was staged to make it appear as if he died, but it was Lucas Mason who perished in the fire. They were in the same year at college and certainly knew each other well. And the important thing was that Lucas was the only child, and his parents were both deceased, so there weren't too many people asking questions. This was Richard Wilson's opportunity to fake his death and take Lucas Mason's place."

"Still, Lucas Mason could have had friends who might wonder about his disappearance," wondered Moretti.

"That's true, but if they tried to contact him and he didn't reply, they probably thought he didn't want to have any contact with them now that he was newly married. The only person who presented a real danger to Richard Wilson was Lucas Mason's future wife. Conveniently, she committed suicide the day he arrived in Miami."

"Richard Wilson killed her because she was the only person in Miami who knew Lucas Mason," affirmed Moretti.

"Exactly."

"You really believe he caused the deaths of his parents?" Moretti questioned. "After all they'd done for him?"

"I'm certain he did. Psychopaths like Richard see adoptive parents as tools to be manipulated and used. Once they've served their purpose, they're discarded. He needed to escape justice, even if it meant sacrificing his family," I explained.

"But he was risking that the police would find out it wasn't his body in the car," Moretti pointed out.

"According to Lee, the fire almost entirely consumed the bodies. And if someone like his brother Robert had claimed it was his family in the car, the police might not have dug deeper," I replied, considering the circumstances.

"Could his brother be involved in all this?" Moretti asked.

"I can't say for sure, but we may have been manipulated from the start," I admitted.

"I don't like getting played," Moretti grumbled.

"The periods during which these horrific crimes were committed in Jacksonville and Miami correspond precisely with those during which the Wilsons were present," I add. "Whether similar crimes were committed during their time in New York remains to be seen."

"I'll ask Wang to check about New York," Moretti said.

"There's something else I'd like to draw your attention to. It's about Nancy Connery."

I explained how she seemed to follow the Wilsons' moves from New York to Jacksonville, then back to New York, and now to Miami.

"It can no longer be a coincidence," I stated.

Moretti's annoyance was evident.

"You might be right about that. Robert Wilson will be here in twenty minutes. Let's see what you can get out of him."

CHAPTER 33

It was the same interrogation room, but the atmosphere felt different this time, as if the stakes were higher, and the tension was palpable. Robert Wilson sat there, no longer under arrest, but with a sense of defiance in his eyes.

"You think you'll be able to get something out of this guy?" John asked, his voice tinged with skepticism.

I glanced at him, uncertainty etched across my face.

"I could be more confident. We have nothing to incriminate him," I admitted.

"Perhaps the fact that we have evidence that his brother is a criminal would unbalance him," he suggested.

"It's a long shot, but it's all we have right now. Let's try to corner him by juggling unexpected questions."

"Yeah. Playing good cop, bad cop," John said, grinning mischievously.

"Exactly."

Taking a deep breath, we entered the room. John walked silently behind me, a reassuring presence ready to support me.

As I faced Wilson, I tried to exude a calm and professional

demeanour, masking my inner turmoil.

"Good morning, Mr. Wilson. We appreciate you taking the time to meet with us," I greeted him politely, maintaining a steady gaze.

Surprisingly, his response was a confident smile. He appeared utterly composed and self-assured. My task ahead would be challenging.

It was hard not to notice his imposing stature, with muscles that could have belonged to a heavyweight boxer.

John activated the recording device, its mechanical voice announcing the date, time, and our identities as the present detectives.

Wilson's eyebrow arched at the sound, a hint of annoyance in his expression.

"Is this necessary?" he inquired, his gaze pointed at the recording device.

"It's a routine procedure to accurately document the information we gather. It aids us in our investigation," I explained briefly, aiming to keep the response concise.

"Very well. Please enlighten me as to why I find myself here once again. Have I been accused of yet another crime?"

Wilson's voice carried a tinge of curiosity as his eyes narrowed slightly.

"It's not about you this time. It's about your brother," John interjected.

The weight of John's statement seemed to settle over the room, taut with tension.

Wilson's look of surprise was palpable, his disbelief evident in his gaze, brows furrowed with confusion and skepticism. He would have convinced the best detective of his sincerity.

"My brother? If this is some joke, it's in deplorable taste," Wilson retorted, his voice a blend of incredulity and frustration.

His emotions played across his features like shadows dancing on the edge of his disbelief.

John probed further, his tone measured, to keep the conversation on track despite the emotional turbulence. "What brings about such a reaction?"

"My brother was tragically killed in a car accident almost two years ago. So, forgive me if I find this line of questioning puzzling," Wilson responded, a layer of pain and defensiveness beneath his words.

I stepped in, my voice maintaining its composed demeanour.

"Are you certain your brother was in the car during that accident?" I asked.

Wilson's response was emphatic, a rush of certainty in his words. "Yes, absolutely certain!"

"In that case," I continued, "how do you explain the discovery of your brother's fingerprints and DNA at the crime scene where Logan Murphy lost his life?"

The question hung in the air.

"Are you talking about the murder that was all over the news?"

He was giving himself time to prepare the answer, I thought.

"Yes, I'm talking about that murder," I agreed.

"Didn't the police identify the murderer as Lucas … something?"

"Lucas Mason. Yes, they did. But your brother's fingerprints and DNA were found at the crime scene."

"I can't explain it. There must be a mistake in your forensic analysis," Wilson shot back. His gaze flickered, momentarily avoiding my steady stare.

"Forensics doesn't lie, Mr. Wilson," I countered, the words gentle but unyielding. "Forensics use cutting-edge scientific techniques to examine and interpret evidence."

"I believe, in this case, they do," Wilson's voice held an edge of defiance.

John, seizing the moment, pivoted the interrogation, steering it toward a new line of questioning.

"Are you acquainted with Logan Murphy?"

"Logan Murphy? I only learned of him through this morning's news," Wilson replied, his tone touched with calculated indifference.

I interjected again, my voice deliberate.

"Are you sure you are not acquainted with Lucas Mason?"

Wilson's brows furrowed, genuine confusion creasing his features, momentarily overshadowing the defensiveness.

"I don't think so. Should I know him?"

"You should," I affirmed, my tone unwavering.

"And why should I know him?"

"Because the individual who assumed the identity of Lucas Mason is your brother, Richard."

"There has to be a mistake,"

John picked up the thread, delving further into the subject.

"Have you had any contact with your brother since the accident?"

"No, I haven't! How could I? He's dead!"

Wilson's retort mixed frustration and exasperation, his veneer slipping slightly. With each passing moment, the suspense deepened, and the struggle to crack Wilson's façade became more pronounced. He rose from his seat, an air of disdain clinging to his movements, an attempt to regain control.

"Mr. Wilson, please understand my colleague's urgency," I interjected softly. "We have substantial evidence indicating your brother is alive and in Miami. We're attempting to comprehend his motives for shadowing you without revealing himself."

"And I'm telling you, Detective, my brother's dead." Wilson's voice held an undertone of desperation. "I saw him and my parents charred by fire in the accident."

"And I understand your position," I acknowledged. "According to the police report, your brother went to pick up your parents in town, and you were waiting for them for dinner. It's perfectly normal to assume that your brother was driving the car. Following your statement, the police did not perform tests to verify the authenticity of the bodies. We believe that, somehow, your brother arranged for Lucas Mason to drive the car, and he was the one charred by fire in the accident."

"And he also managed to cause the accident and kill our parents and Lucas Mason! Very inventive. And what would be his reason for doing so?" he exclaimed in a frustrated voice.

"Richard's girlfriend had been murdered," answered John in a steady voice. "And your brother was considered the primary suspect. He faked his death to avoid justice."

"First of all, my brother had a rock-solid alibi proving that he wasn't the one who killed his girlfriend. Second, my brother would never hurt our parents. And third, he was smart, but not smart enough to pull this off."

Wilson's defence was swift.

"Maybe he had some help." John's accusation hung in the air.

"What are you implying?"

"Secrets enslave us, Mr. Wilson," replied John. It's time to set yourself free."

"I don't know what game you're playing." Wilson's tone hardened. "But this is harassment. Moving forward, any inquiries you have should be directed to my lawyer. Consider yourselves fortunate I'm not pursuing legal action against you."

John's accusation had shifted the dynamics. A

miscalculated move. Now that Robert Wilson knew of police suspicion, he would be guarded, making it harder to discern guilt. Reluctantly, we had no choice but to release him from the interrogation.

Throughout the session, I observed Wilson closely, noting the subtlety of his body language and the deviations from his usual comportment. His swift replies, lacking the customary contemplation, whispered of concealed truths.

One undeniable conclusion remained with the culmination of the interrogation: Wilson's words held more than they revealed. The truth lay buried, waiting to be unearthed.

CHAPTER 34

My gut told me that everyone who had followed the interrogation had come to the same conclusion: Robert Wilson was hiding something. Whether he was involved in the crimes himself or protecting his brother remained to be seen.

"Good job, both of you," praised Moretti. "This individual is unquestionably guilty. Even though he's so in control of his emotions, he would have convinced any detective without experience of his sincerity."

"Thank you, Sergeant," John responded.

"It is rare to encounter a scenario where a twin, linked by an indestructible bond, shows no curiosity about the fate of his ostensibly deceased brother," I said.

"I agree," said Moretti. "Even if there was only a faint hope that his brother was alive, he should have clung to that hope."

"That's because he was determined to convince us that his brother is dead," said John.

"Have there been any developments in the BOLO search for his brother?" I inquired.

"Regrettably, no substantial progress so far," Moretti admitted. "The uncanny resemblance between these twins has prompted a deluge of tips and calls, predominantly identifying the individual as Robert Wilson. On the other hand, Wang has some important information, so go see him!"

Lee usually had a talent for unearthing important information. I hoped this was the case because we needed more to go on with Richard Wilson in the wind.

We found Lee pounding away on the keyboard. His face radiated with an air of accomplishment as he addressed us.

"Gentlemen, I have uncovered noteworthy information. Are you prepared for the revelations that lie ahead?"

"We're all ears," I affirmed.

"As per your request, I undertook a comparative analysis of the criminal patterns in New York, Miami, and Jacksonville," he began. "What I discovered is remarkable: the modus operandi of the crimes was conspicuously akin across these locations. Moreover, the timing of these criminal acts corresponded precisely to the period during which the Wilson family resided in New York. Strikingly, no comparable incidents were reported after their relocation to Miami."

Lee was a great scholar and never missed an opportunity to demonstrate his excellence in Shakespeare's language, Latin, or any other language he knew.

"However," he continued, underscoring the depth of his findings. "There is more to this intricate puzzle. Prepare to be astounded. The residence inhabited by Richard Wilson, also known as Lucas Mason, is owned by the Sunshine Build Group."

It was becoming increasingly clear that the motive behind Richard Wilson's impersonation of Lucas Mason was not only the fact that they were both surgical assistants. The connection to Sunshine Build Group, and then undoubtedly with Harry Miller and his family, overshadowed the coincidence of their qualification.

"This case is becoming increasingly complex," said John.

"It's looking that way."

"We'll have to explore any possible links between Richard Wilson and Harry Miller's family."

"We should start by interviewing Richard Wilson's alias Lucas Mason hospital colleagues," I suggested. "And then we need to methodically interview everyone at Sunshine Build Group we haven't had a chance to speak with yet."

"We should ask Moretti to put a tail on Robert Wilson in case his brother tries to contact him," suggested John.

"I believe Robert Wilson knows exactly where his brother is hiding."

"He's innocent until proven guilty," John said while heading to the garage.

"It'll be hard to prove one or the other," I concluded.

"Let's take a breather," John suggested with a wry smile. "I think this is the perfect time for a lunch break. We've got a long day ahead, and I perform much better on a full stomach."

We veered into a deli chain, grabbing a generous platter of sandwiches and salads before settling on a bench outside.

The day embodied the quintessential Florida scene; the gentle breeze off the Atlantic was a soothing caress, while laughter and the distant sound of music intertwined with the ocean's rhythm.

"It's rather refreshing hearing the carefree laughter of happy people, isn't it?" John remarked, nodding toward the sun-soaked beachgoers.

"That's why we pursue individuals like Richard Wilson, or should I say, Lucas Mason," I replied thoughtfully. "To ensure that people can continue revelling in that happiness."

We savoured the last bites of our meal, the flavours mingling with the salty air, and soon found ourselves at the hospital's information desk.

After consulting the information desk for directions, we arrived at the surgery department's reception area. A middle-aged woman with greying hair was sitting behind the counter.

"Can I be of assistance?" she asked in a gravelly voice.

We promptly displayed our badges.

"We'd appreciate a word with the attending surgeon," John stated.

Regrettably, the woman shook her head.

"Dr. Kaminsky is currently in the operating room."

"Do you know how long he'll be?" I asked.

"If all proceeds according to plan, he should be available in a few minutes. Follow the corridor, and you'll find the waiting room."

"Thank you," I said courteously.

Inside the waiting room, only three individuals sat, their expressions etched with anxiety. Their attention was fixed on the closed door, beyond which a significant operation was underway.

The scene invoked an involuntary shiver; hospital waiting rooms, to me, symbolized the weight of unsettling news, the uncertainty of someone's well-being.

I watched the anxious faces of those awaiting the result of the operation, and a haunting memory resurfaced: the hours I had spent in a room like this, fervently wishing for my mother's safe return from the operating table. It was a feeling I could never thoroughly shake off.

Luckily, we didn't have to wait long. A man clad in surgical scrubs and a mask emerged, cradling a cup. There was a hint of a smile as he addressed the trio who had risen in anticipation of his report. He was delivering good news.

Once the private moment concluded, we approached him, presented our badges, and explained the reason for our presence.

"I was shocked when I caught wind of the news," he admitted, his voice tinged with surprise. "Lucas Mason was an exceptional assistant, the best I've ever had. While my interactions with him were limited to the surgical suite, I would never have anticipated his connection to such a criminal act."

"Is there anything you can recall that might assist our investigation?" asked John.

"I wish I could provide insight," he responded. "But I can't. As I told you, my interactions with him were limited to the medical sphere. Perhaps another member of the team could offer you more valuable information."

A clear pattern emerged after several hours of interviews with the team members; Richard Wilson alias Lucas Mason had been a reserved individual, shrouded in privacy. There were no notable connections with his colleagues; his professional life was distinct from his personal life.

We were left with the knowledge we had begun with, a frustrating loop of limited information.

However, the tides were about to change.

CHAPTER 35

The sun was high and hot, hammering down mercilessly when we left the hospital. We headed back to the car, our minds buzzing with the puzzle. The interviews had left us with more questions than answers, but one thing was clear: Richard Wilson, alias Lucas Mason, was a complex enigma. I couldn't shake the frustration of thinking that the killers had done their homework better than us.

John noticed my contemplative state.

"Lost in thought?" he asked, keeping his eyes on the road.

I nodded. "Yeah, just trying to piece together all the information we gathered today. In the meantime, more people are in danger."

John glanced at me, a knowing look in his eyes.

"I feel the same. We need to dig deeper into Richard Wilson's background, find out what he was up to outside of work."

"Yeah..."

Back at headquarters, we spread out the collected evidence and notes.

"Okay. Let's find out about Richard Wilson's personal

life," I suggested. "We need to know who he associated with outside of work, his habits, and any potential conflicts."

John nodded, his fingers dancing over the keyboard as he searched for leads.

"Here's something interesting," he said, pointing to the screen. "A social media account linked to Lucas Mason, but it's private."

"We need to get access to that," I said.

"Let's talk to Lee. I don't think he'll have difficulty breaking into Mason's social media account."

Lee's help proved invaluable, and within ten minutes, we gained access to Mason's private social media account.

The information we found was enlightening and baffling: photos of places he had visited, cryptic messages, and connections to certain people. One name stood out: Cassandra Simpson. More digging revealed that she'd been his girlfriend for some time.

"I think we've found our missing link," John said, his eyes alight with excitement. "She might know more about Mason than anybody else."

We contacted Cassandra Simpson and scheduled a meeting at her apartment. Cassandra's guarded eyes and cautious demeanour were hard to miss as we settled onto the sofa.

"Lucas was troubled," she confessed, her voice hinting of reluctance. "But he never opened up to me much. The last time we spoke, he seemed distant, obsessed with something he called *the truth*."

"The truth about what?" I inquired.

She hesitated, then finally broke her silence.

"He mentioned something about people ruining others' lives, secrets within wealthy families in Miami."

"Did he ever explain the details or mention any names?" I probed.

"No, I didn't press him for more information," she admitted. "There was something in his eyes that frightened me."

"Did he introduce you to any friends or acquaintances?" I asked, hopeful for a lead.

"He was a very private person," Cassandra replied. "We only dated for three months, and the only person I knew of was Mrs. Veronica Hernandez, a cleaning lady from the hospital. He needed a housekeeper, and I recommended her."

"Did he hire her?" I inquired.

"Yes, he did," Cassandra affirmed. "And she was genuinely grateful. She and her family arrived from Cuba a year ago, and she worked tirelessly to secure a better future for her children. But lately, she's been avoiding me, and I can't blame her."

"We need her address and phone number," I requested.

She shot me a puzzled look.

"I know it might seem intrusive," I continued, "but we only want to apprehend a criminal. She may possess vital information that could aid our investigation. She'll understand you had no choice but to share her details with us."

"I only have her phone number," she said, scrambling it on a piece of paper.

"Do you know her work schedule at the hospital?" John inquired.

"She's not working today," Cassandra explained. "She typically only works at the hospital for three days. This is the reason I recommended her to Lucas. She needed the money."

"Thank you for your cooperation, Miss Simpson," I said, slipping my business card onto the table. "If you recall anything else that might be of assistance, please don't hesitate to reach out."

With Veronica Hernandez's phone number in hand,

obtaining her address was straightforward. Thirty-eight minutes later, we stood at her apartment door. We heard approaching footsteps, and a woman emerged in the doorway, dressed in a green jumpsuit that seemed to swallow her petite frame. Her coal-black eyes surveyed us from head to toe.

"Yes?" she inquired.

"Are you Mrs. Veronica Hernandez?" John asked.

"Yes," she confirmed. "And who are you?"

We presented our badges, catching her by surprise.

"I'm Detective Olsen, and this is Detective Freeman," John introduced. "We'd like to ask you a few questions. May we come in?"

"If this is about our immigration documents, we are legal in this country," she stated.

"We are aware of that, Mrs. Hernandez," John reassured her. "Our visit is unrelated to those documents."

"Alright, then. Come in."

Inside her modestly furnished apartment, she gestured for us to sit on the sofa as she sat on a nearby chair.

"Mrs. Hernandez," I began, "we understand that you worked as a cleaning lady for Lucas Mason."

She looked at me with wide, fearful eyes, and a long silence lingered before she finally responded.

"Yes, I did."

"With the accusations against Lucas Mason, we are investigating several crimes," I explained. "Is there anything you observed or heard while working at his house that might assist our investigation?"

Again, her gaze held a deep fear, and her body language hinted at concealed knowledge.

"No, I don't think so," she replied hesitantly. "I cleaned Mr. Mason's house on Thursdays during his hospital hours. I believe your inquiries might be fruitless."

The unease in her eyes and her defensive demeanour

suggested she was hiding something. John and I exchanged knowing glances, both recognizing the signs.

"Mrs. Hernandez," John said gently, "you don't need to be afraid. We can ensure your safety and that of your family."

"Think about all the lives this psychopath has taken," I added. "You didn't leave your home country to live in fear in Miami. Help us put him behind bars."

She sighed, and a touch of panic crept into her voice.

"At first, Mr. Mason seemed like the most respectful and charming person I'd ever met," she began. "Until three weeks ago."

"What happened then?" John inquired.

"I wasn't feeling well that Thursday, so I decided to postpone my cleaning day to Friday, thinking he'd be at work as usual," she recounted. "I made the mistake of not notifying him of the change."

"What happened that Friday?" I asked.

"I was cleaning one of the bathrooms when I heard voices in the living room. I didn't expect Mr. Mason to return home so soon, especially with visitors. I prepared to announce myself when the conversation in the living room grew heated.

"Did you hear what they were saying?"

"Yes."

"Can you tell us what it was about?"

"I will try. I heard a woman's authoritative voice say, 'I don't want you to act alone. You must adhere to my plans. Do you understand?' She was addressing Mr. Mason. 'Yes, Mom, I understand,' Mr. Mason replied."

"Mom?" I echoed. "As far as we know, he's an orphan."

"Exactly," Mrs. Hernandez agreed. "When we first met, Mr. Mason gave me the impression that he came from a wealthy family, but he later revealed his parents were both deceased and that the house belonged to a distant relative."

"What did you do when you realized they didn't know you were there?" John inquired.

"I initially intended to announce myself," she confessed, "but I became so anxious that I retreated to a corner of the living room. That's when I noticed there was another man with them. He bore such a striking resemblance to Mr. Mason that, for a moment, I believed I was hallucinating. Just then, they left the house."

John and I exchanged glances, now sure of the man's identity.

"So, they didn't see you," John observed.

"No," Mrs. Hernandez confirmed. "I was so relieved that I promised myself never to change my workday without informing him."

"Can you describe the woman for us?" I inquired.

From her description, it became clear that the woman Lucas Mason referred to as his mother was none other than Nancy Connery. However, I needed confirmation.

"Mrs. Hernandez, do you have a computer?" I asked.

"My son has a laptop," she replied. "Why do you ask?"

"Would you mind if I use it for a moment?" I requested.

"Not at all," she replied, retrieving the laptop from her son's room.

I swiftly typed Nancy Connery's name into a search engine and located several photographs. I turned the screen toward Mrs. Hernandez.

"Is this the woman you saw in Lucas Mason's house?" I inquired.

"Yes. How did you know?" she inquired.

"Your information has proven invaluable to our investigation," I replied, evading her question. "Thank you. I'll leave you my card in case you remember anything else."

I signalled to John that it was time to depart.

"Finally," John remarked as we exited the apartment. "All

the puzzle pieces are coming together. You were right to trust your instincts about Nancy Connery. We should have asked Mrs. Hernandez if she'd be willing to testify?"

"First, she's too frightened for herself and her family to testify in court. And second, Nancy Connery and Robert Wilson have too good of lawyers. They'll tear Mrs. Hernandez apart."

"What do you suggest then?"

"I don't know yet; I have to think."

We left Mrs. Hernandez's apartment building smiling, thinking we'd finally start to see the light at the end of the tunnel.

CHAPTER 36

When we arrived back at headquarters, the sun painted the city in shades of orange. Moretti was in his office, and we wasted no time giving him a rundown of our day.

"Great job!" he commended us, his enthusiasm evident. "Now we're certain that Robert Wilson is his brother's partner in crime. And needless to say, this puts Nancy Connery squarely under the microscope. Tomorrow morning, I'll compel her to take a DNA test."

"Apologies, Sergeant," I interjected, "but I'm not sure that's a good idea."

Moretti raised an eyebrow.

"Why not?"

"Even if DNA proves she's their mother, we can't accuse her of any crime," I explained. "She could argue that she had no idea that Robert and Richard Wilson were her children, that she hadn't seen her children since they had been adopted. She might claim that Mrs. Hernandez mistook her for someone else."

"But we have Mrs. Hernandez as a witness!" Moretti countered.

"As I told John," I began, "Mrs. Hernandez is too terrified for herself and her family to testify in court. And even if we subpoena her to testify, you know as well as I do that Nancy Connery and Robert Wilson have formidable lawyers. They'd tear Mrs. Hernandez apart."

"What about the fact that the periods during which these horrific crimes were committed in Jacksonville, New York, and Miami align precisely with the times the Wilsons were present?" John suggested. "We have evidence that these crimes commenced each time they relocated to a new city."

"And Nancy Connery seems to have tracked the Wilsons' movements from New York to Jacksonville, back to New York, and now to Miami," I added.

"Exactly," John affirmed.

"We still don't have enough. There are no prints, no DNA, and our sole witness is deceased. Our only viable charge is against Richard Wilson, who poss as Lucas Mason, and he's vanished."

"She's right," Moretti sighed, a look of frustration crossing his face. "Even if Mrs. Hernandez testifies, we can only accuse Nancy Connery and Robert Wilson of harbouring a suspect. Harbouring a suspect or a wanted fugitive in a criminal investigation is a crime, but fourteen states offer family member exemptions. Unfortunately, Florida is one of those states that allows this. We need more concrete evidence to charge them with the crimes."

"To sum it up," I began, "somehow Nancy Connery managed to reconnect with her sons after their adoption, and they've been in constant contact ever since."

"Do you think she could have participated in the crimes?" asked John.

I nodded. "I'm sure of it. According to Tom, the blood spatter patterns indicate that there were likely two killers involved—one over 6 feet tall and the other just 5.41 feet tall. Both Wilson brothers are over six feet tall, but Nancy Connery is no more than five feet and four inches tall.”

“It can’t be a coincidence that Robert Wilson works for Sunshine Build Group while his brother lives in a house owned by the same company,” Moretti said.

“There must be a connection with Harry Miller and his family,” John suggested.

“The connection is clear,” replied Moretti. “And what’s also clear is that they planned these crimes meticulously. I’ll ask Wang to dig deeper into their pasts.”

“I still believe that the Miller family members were killed for revenge,” I added. “We must uncover the reason, the connection between them and the brothers.”

“But how do we prove all this?” asked John.

“It’s going to take time and hard work,” sighed Moretti. “In the meantime, they could disappear just as Richard Wilson did. That’s why I may have to subpoena Mrs. Hernandez and try to frame them for harbouring a criminal. It will buy us some time.”

“I have a suspicion that Richard Wilson may not have truly left town,” I ventured to say.

“What leads you to believe that?” asked John.

“Well, after we issued the BOLO for Richard Wilson, his brother boldly exposed himself publicly to test the reaction time of both the police and the general public. They bear such a striking resemblance that it’s nearly impossible to tell them apart. Now that they’re aware of the difficulty in leaving town undetected, it’s doubtful he’d make a hasty exit,” I explained. “Perhaps he had already left town before we issued the BOLO,” John suggested.

“I believe he required more time to plan his departure. Let’s not forget that the BOLO was issued just a few hours after he abandoned Logan Murphy’s car in the mall parking lot,” I asserted confidently.

"He may have friends helping him stay hidden," John proposed.

"Friends might not be willing to harbour a criminal, but family often will. Nancy Connery's home could be the safest place for him to hide. If my hunch is correct, not even the most skilled lawyer in the world will be able to help them," I concluded.

"That's a possibility," Moretti conceded. "However, even if Richard Wilson is inside the house, the legal hurdle is that we'd need a warrant to enter. I'll have to convince the judge to issue one based on the latest information, and he'll likely want us to be certain Richard Wilson is there."

"If that's what he requires, we don't have a choice but to respect his request," John assured him.

"Alright then," Moretti concluded, "let's hope we can catch this cold-blooded killer. I'll arrange for a discreet surveillance team to monitor her house."

"If you don't mind, I'd prefer to lead the surveillance myself," I volunteered.

"I'll join her," John added, excitement etched on his face.

Moretti nodded. "Then it's settled."

"Is it possible to use the Range-R device to determine how many people are inside the house?" I asked, hoping he would say yes.

"Unfortunately, no," Moretti sighed. "I'd need Captain Morales' approval to use the device, and he won't grant it based on mere assumptions. However, you can wear audio transmitters so you're in constant contact with the team, and they can listen in."

"Okay then," I said, turning to John. "Let's get to work."

We spent the next half-hour briefing the team on the situation and what we expected of them. As we left headquarters, night was falling over the city.

Nancy Connery's residence was in Shenandoah, a

neighbourhood strategically located just minutes from every crucial part of the city. It was a short stroll from Miami Beach, Coconut Grove, Brickell, and downtown Miami. On a balmy summer day, the scent of the ocean wafted through the air. The house wasn't grand but sprawled over a spacious plot with numerous palm trees.

Across the street, a flower shop stood closed at this hour. We parked the van in a nearby lot, and the wait began.

One by one, the lights in neighbouring houses dimmed, and I began to feel the caffeine saturation in my system. But there was still light in Nancy Connery's home.

Fatigue began to set in among the team members, and the atmosphere inside the van grew oppressive.

"It's maddening to be so close and powerless to check if a criminal is inside," John muttered.

"The law applies to everyone," one team member chimed in. "Until we're certain he's inside, we must abide by it."

That's when I made a decision that could have jeopardized my career.

"I'm going to check it out," I announced.

"Liv, you're out of your mind!" John exclaimed. "Can you imagine the consequences if…"

Without waiting for him to finish, I quietly closed the van door and approached Nancy Connery's residence, sticking to the shadows as much as possible. I spent some time concealed behind a palm tree before silently inching closer to the illuminated window.

As I neared the window, I heard the front door swing open abruptly, and Nancy Connery's voice filled the night air.

"Don't come any closer. I'm armed."

I realized she must have a motion-activated home security camera that records and sends alerts. Her voice trembled with a mix of fear and authority.

"She possesses a firearm," John's voice transmitted

discreetly through my audio device. "We are prepared to intervene."

"No, please hold and observe," I murmured while covertly securing my audio transmitter beneath my clothing.

Simultaneously, Nancy Connery advanced, her firearm directed at me.

"Detective Olsen," she articulated, her tone tinged with surprise. "What brings you to my garden at this hour? Are the police spying on me?"

"I know Richard Wilson is your son. While the police may not entertain suspicions of your involvement in his crimes, I do," I responded with unwavering conviction, trusting that she would believe I acted alone.

"Will observing me through the window substantiate your claims?" she inquired.

"Indeed, if you're harbouring your criminal son within this residence. Subsequently, I can present compelling evidence to the police."

"I'm perplexed by your insinuations," she retorted, though her countenance betrayed relief.

My ruse had convinced her that I was acting independently.

"Very well," she pressed on. "Let's see if you are right," she said, gesturing for me to enter.

She promptly disarmed me upon gaining access, claiming my sidearm from its holster. Fortunately, she hadn't noticed that I had an audio transmitter beneath my clothing.

I followed her without uttering a word and found myself unsurprised to discover the two Wilson brothers seated side by side on the sofa.

The striking resemblance between the two brothers struck me like a bolt of lightning. They stood there, silently observing me, their eyes brimming with amusement like two puppets expertly manipulated by the same unseen hand. A sudden shiver coursed up my spine.

"Hello, Detective," one of them finally spoke, breaking the eerie silence. "It's always a pleasure seeing you."

So, he was Robert.

"Mom, are you sure she came all alone?" inquired Richard.

"Of course, I'm sure. Otherwise, her colleagues would have rushed to her aid when I pointed the gun at her. I'd still like to check if she's wearing a wire."

With her gun pointed at me, she approached and lifted my clothes. If she discovered the audio transmitter, I would lose contact with John and the team. Fortunately, as she lifted my clothes and exposed my stomach and breasts, she pushed the transmitter between the folds of my clothes.

"You see, I was right; the idiot came on her own," she declared triumphantly.

"You're always right, Mom," the two brothers chimed in unison.

Witnessing these grown men regress to obedient children in the presence of their mother was nothing short of fascinating.

"Wow," I remarked, trying to keep my voice steady. You've done quite the job with your sons."

"Do you know that you can desensitize a child through the practice of violent behaviour?" she replied, shrugging nonchalantly.

"That makes sense. Is that what you did when you finally found your sons?"

"Yes," she admitted, her gaze flickering toward the brothers. "And they've excelled at it. Remember when I taught you how to take a puppy's life?" she asked the brothers.

"Yeah, Mom," both brothers replied in eerie unison. "We do."

"You've trained them well."

"Haven't I?" she mused with a sinister grin. "I even let Richard handle the last kill on his own."

"How many have you done together?" I ventured, unable to suppress my morbid curiosity.

"Ah, the detective in you," she chuckled softly. "Even when you know you won't leave here alive, you can't resist asking questions. Very well, I'll tell you how many people we've killed: not enough."

"Why do you encourage your sons to commit such heinous acts?" I pressed on.

"I don't encourage them," she retorted. "They derive pleasure from it."

"I do," Robert interjected, his voice dripping with malice as he approached me, locking eyes with mine. "I have fond memories of the crimes committed with my mother and brother, especially when they're personal."

"Are you referring to the Miller family?" I probed, praying that John and the team, who were listening, wouldn't storm in prematurely, robbing me of vital answers.

"Yes, Harry Miller and his family were as personal as it gets."

"Why?" I inquired, my eagerness to unravel their twisted motives intensifying.

"Because he's the father of my two boys," Nancy Connery confessed with a cold detachment. "I was only sixteen when I fell in love with him. He promised we'd conquer the world together, that he would remove all competition by fighting like a Viking, and become the owner of a large construction company. But he abandoned me when he learned I was pregnant. I followed his career, and he did fight like a Viking, but not for me, and not for his two boys."

"Now I understand why you emulated the brutal Viking 'Bloodeagle' ritual in his death," I mused.

"You're more astute than I gave you credit for, Detective," she acknowledged. "I yearned to get my hands on him, watch him squirm, and savour the scent of fear that emanated from his every pore. And when I did, I'd raise a sharp scalpel, letting him anticipate the excruciating agony while reminding him that I, a stronger Viking, had my two sons to aid me."

"But why did you kill his son and his wife?" I inquired.

"They took the place that only my children and I were entitled to."

"And Briana Cooper, she was in the wrong place at the wrong time," I concluded.

"That's correct. I hired her under the guise of being Harry's wife, suspecting his infidelity."

"And naturally, you killed Gloria Perez because she had witnessed your faces."

"I must admit, I took great pleasure in slitting that young woman's throat," Richard said.

"Did you ever think she had her whole life ahead of her?" I asked.

"I wished the lesson had lasted longer and been more agonizing, but time was of the essence," he replied.

"You performed admirably, Richard," Nancy Connery commended. "I'm proud of you."

"Thank you, Mom."

"Was Logan Murphy your accomplice?" I questioned.

"That imbecile! He fit perfectly into our plan. Making him look guilty was child's play."

"What about the murders you committed in Jacksonville and New York? Did you have specific motives for your victims, or was it purely random?"

"They were all guilty of abandoning their children in orphanages, thinking their guilt could be absolved with a hefty donation."

"Given your traumatic childhood with a criminal father, I would have thought that you might have detested crime."

"I cherished every moment by my father's side," Nancy Connery replied, her eyes glinting with a twisted nostalgia.

"I relished each second as he dismembered his victims. The cold basement and the warmth of blood spilling from their wounds intoxicated me. The scent of blood, it's a drug I can't resist."

"Like a predatory animal."

"Enough talk," she declared, returning to the brothers. "It's time."

She approached me and pointed her gun at me.

"Yeah, guys, it's time," I echoed, silently urging John and the team to grasp my hidden message. I needed to prolong this dialogue to give them time to break inside.

"Robert, tie her up and use the same scalpel you used on your father," Nancy instructed.

"Why do you let your mother dictate your actions, Robert?" I interjected.

"She doesn't dictate," Robert stammered.

"Stop listening to her, Robert," Nancy Connery commanded.

"Sorry, Mom."

"I thought you were acting independently," I continued to press.

"I do."

"Clearly," I prodded further. "I've seen your mother telling you what to do when she's present. You become a mere child in her presence."

"Finish it, Robert," said an impatient Nancy Connery.

"Yeah, Robert, listen to your mother," I urged, anxiously waiting for the door to swing open any second for John and the team to rescue me.

"Shut up!" Robert exploded. "I'm going to dismember you and bury you in the Everglades beneath twelve feet of mud."

In that harrowing moment, the door burst open, and John led the charge, the team trailing closely behind, weapons at the ready.

CHAPTER 37

Ihadn't slept much that night and was woozy when Moretti told John and me to follow him into Captain Morales' office. "I hope he'll offer us coffee; I need it badly," I whispered to John.

"I suppose he will. Today, you're the hero."

He was right. When we entered his office, Captain Morales asked us if we wanted coffee.

"First of all," he said, "I want to congratulate the two of you on your outstanding detective work. I know this case hasn't been easy for either of you. But you stuck with it and brought it to a successful conclusion."

"Thank you, Captain," John and I said almost simultaneously.

There was a moment of silence, and then Moretti cleared his throat.

"We have a problem. Robert Wilson has cancer. They took him to hospital because he was vomiting blood."

"Even cancer isn't punishment enough for all his crimes," said John. "He should die by lethal injection or electrocution to look into the eyes of death."

"I agree with you," answered Moretti. "But the law and humanity must prevail, regardless of our personal feelings," Moretti continued, with a heaviness in his voice. "And now, with this diagnosis, this case becomes even more complicated."

"What do you mean by complicated?" asked John. We have him; we have the evidence. His diagnosis shouldn't change anything."

Moretti sighed.

"Legal complications. His lawyers will use his illness as a way to garner sympathy. They might argue that he is no longer a threat and should be allowed a compassionate release."

"That's absurd!" I exclaimed. "After everything he's done?"

Moretti raised his hand, gesturing for calm.

"I'm not saying I agree with it, Detective Olsen. But we must be prepared for any potential tactics they might employ."

The tension in the room was palpable. I took a deep breath, trying to contain my emotions.

"So, what's our next move?" I asked.

"We keep doing our jobs," Moretti responded, determination evident in his eyes. "We ensure our evidence is rock solid and there are no loopholes for them to exploit. And you two need to prepare for court, testify, and ensure the world knows the monster Robert Wilson truly is."

John nodded in agreement.

"His illness shouldn't absolve him of his crimes," concluded Moretti. "He needs to face justice, one way or another. Now, let's get to work. There's much to be done."

In the days that followed, we prepared to testify in court to prove beyond a doubt that the two Wilson brothers and their mother were among the most dangerous criminals Miami had ever known. Our job was challenging because, however hideous the details, there was nothing we could say about the case that hadn't already been endlessly regurgitated on the news.

However, the more evidence I accumulated, the more convinced I became that the jury would give the correct verdict. Our evidence would prove to them that people capable of such atrocious crimes could only be monsters, so much an offence against human decency and compassion. Monsters who need to be punished. Permanently."

The trial had erupted into a full-blown media frenzy. Television trucks and news vans clogged the streets, creating a chaotic spectacle. A horde of familiar faces, armed with cameras and microphones, descended upon us when we stepped out of the courtroom where Nancy Connery and her sons had been unanimously sentenced to death.

We paid little attention to the clamour, deliberately leaving space for Moretti to seize the spotlight and praise the exceptional efforts of the police.

"Did you witness that?" John exclaimed, his voice tinged with disbelief. "Those killers did not react during the trial!"

"I did," I replied, my gaze still fixed on the retreating figures of Nancy Connery and her sons. "One of the most challenging aspects of my work is during these trials when the victims' families stand before the court to bear their souls, shedding tears … and there those criminals sat, motionless, refusing to acknowledge their presence. It's as though their words meant nothing to them. It's as if … there's a void behind those eyes. I find it impossible to master compassion for these murderers, let alone forgiveness."

John nodded solemnly.

"Well, no matter how tirelessly we work, there always seems to be another life lost," he said. "But if we can apprehend as many of these killers as possible, we can make the world safer."

At that moment, the crowd gave Moretti quite an ovation, and we knew it was time to return to headquarters. At this time of the day, it was an easy drive back. Because this high-profile case had been settled, the conference room filled quickly, with everyone eager to share in the success. With a satisfied expression, Moretti crossed the room.

"Our job is to protect and serve," he said. "And in this case, we've done our job well. I want to thank Detectives Olsen and Freeman for all their hard work. They spent countless hours working on this high-profile case, chasing leads, and sifting through evidence to bring this to a close finally."

Applause and cheers filled the conference room as John and I exchanged proud smiles. The sense of accomplishment was palpable in the room. As the celebration continued, Moretti gestured for everyone to quiet down so he could speak.

"Now, it's time to unwind a bit. We've earned it," he announced, eliciting cheers of agreement. "I know a great place just down the beach, a bar with a spectacular ocean view. Let's head there and raise our glasses to a job well done!"

Everybody quickly gathered their belongings and exited the conference room, excitedly chatting about their plans for the evening.

As we strolled down the beach, the salty breeze and the waves crashing against the shore added to the sense of relaxation and accomplishment.

Soon, we arrived at the beachside bar, adorned with twinkling string lights and lively music playing in the background. We found a long table with a prime view of the sunset over the horizon, and everyone settled in, ordering their drinks of choice.

When the drinks arrived, Moretti raised his glass.

"To teamwork, dedication, and justice served!" he toasted, and the clinking of glasses echoed throughout the bar.

The evening unfolded with laughter, stories from

past cases, and well-deserved relaxation. It was a night to remember, a celebration of our hard work and commitment to upholding the law.

As the sun dipped below the horizon, casting vibrant hues across the sky, I couldn't help but feel a deep sense of relief. We had done it, and it was over.

"Take the weekend off, Detective Olsen," Moretti said, giving my arm a reassuring pat. "You deserve it."

"Thank you, Sergeant," I replied, savouring the last bite of cheese pizza on my plate.

By the time we wrapped up, it was already past ten, and I found myself at Jensen's doorstep. He swung the door open, enfolding me in his embrace. I inhaled deeply, relishing his clean, refreshing scent.

Dressed in a white T-shirt and jeans, his hair still slightly damp from a recent shower, Jensen exuded an undeniable magnetism that never failed to spark our connection.

"Hi," he murmured, kissing me softly beneath my earlobe. "Did you have a good evening?"

"I did, and I scored a weekend off work. Happy?"

"Very. You deserve a break."

"Right now, I deserve a shower."

"Can I join you?"

"I was hoping you'd ask."

Moments later, the water enveloped us, and we gasped and moaned, swept away by the intensity of our passion.

"I want to feel all of you," Jensen whispered against my skin.

I attempted to lift myself off him playfully, but he held me firmly.

"No, don't move, just feel."

I surrendered to the exquisite sensation, my desire igniting, hot and heavy, deep within me. I threw my head back and let out a strangled cry of pure pleasure.

The night wore on, and we finally succumbed to sleep, our bodies utterly spent.

The aroma of bacon and eggs greeted me as I awoke the following day, filling me with a sense of contentment as I contemplated the two days ahead with Jensen.

"Good morning," Jensen greeted me with a warm smile.

"Good morning," I replied, basking in his cheerful demeanour.

I settled into a chair, propped my hands behind my head, and enjoyed the view: Jensen preparing breakfast, dressed only in jeans and barefoot, a sight that never failed to captivate me.

"I didn't want to wake you," he said, "but we've been invited by Carlos, John's brother, to spend the weekend with him and his wife on their boat. But if you're not up for it, I can tell him we have other plans."

I immediately realized that I hadn't shared the details of our relationship with anyone, unsure if it was more than a flirtation. Carlos would undoubtedly inform his brother, John. However, if Jensen were willing to introduce me to his best friend, my worries about John discovering our affair would vanish.

"I'd love to spend two days on a boat," I replied, longing for sun and seawater after the recent stress. "I'm as pale as a ghost."

"It's settled then. I'll call Carlos. Are you an experienced scuba diver?"

"I've tried it a few times, but I'm not an expert. And I don't have a suit."

"No worries, we'll stop and pick one up. I'll let Carlos know we might be a little late."

"What about food?"

We don't need to buy anything. Carlos just told me they have everything we'll need."

After swinging by my apartment to grab some swimsuits and clothes, we quickly stopped to purchase a diving suit and all the necessary gear.

It was a glorious day, and the marina buzzed with activity as boats prepared to set sail. I was astounded by the size and elegance of Carlos' boat.

"Wow," I remarked to Jensen. "Your friend Carlos must be quite well-off to have a boat like this."

"He's doing all right. We've had some good contracts this past year."

"Still, how much can someone pay you to rescue a kidnapped person?"

"Well, think about how much someone would pay us to save their child when the kidnappers demand fifty million for their release."

"Hello, mate," greeted a burly man as he stepped off the boat to meet us. He was dressed only in shorts, and his black skin glistened with sun lotion. He shook Jensen's hand before turning to me.

"You must be Liv. My brother speaks very highly of you."

"Hi," I said, shaking his hand.

"Come, I'd like you to meet my wife, Miranda."

We followed him onto the boat, and a petite, attractive brunette rushed over and greeted Jensen warmly.

"And who's this beautiful young woman?" she asked, her attention shifting to me.

"Her name is Liv, and she's my girlfriend," said Jensen.

"Ah! Finally! I thought you were going to die a celibate. Come, I'll show you to your cabin."

As we set sail, the sun bathed us in its warm embrace, and the gentle sway of the boat immediately lulled us into a state of relaxation. Carlos and Miranda wasted no time in making us feel at home. They were a charming couple and shared a deep love for each other.

Our first stop was a secluded cove with crystal-clear waters, a haven for scuba diving enthusiasts. Jensen and I eagerly donned our diving gear and ventured beneath the surface.

The underwater world was a mesmerizing tapestry of vibrant coral, exotic fish, and serenity that only the deep ocean could offer. We held hands and explored the colourful marine life, our smiles hidden behind our masks.

After an exhilarating dive, we returned to the boat, where Miranda had prepared a sumptuous seafood feast. Freshly caught lobster, grilled shrimp, and a medley of exotic salads graced the table. We indulged in the delicious spread, savouring our hosts' flavours and company.

When the day drifted into evening, we found ourselves lounging on the boat's deck, sipping cocktails and watching the sunset paint the sky with hues of orange and pink. It was a moment of pure serenity, and I couldn't have asked for a more perfect setting to be with Jensen.

Our second day on the boat was even more adventurous. Carlos, an avid water sports enthusiast, had various toys, from jet skis to paddleboards.

We started the morning with heart-pounding jet skiing, racing each other across the shimmering sea.

After our thrilling water escapades, we anchored at a secluded beach accessible only by boat. The soft, powdery sand invited us to relax, and we spent the afternoon swimming and strolling hand in hand along the shore.

We set off for another scuba diving expedition in the late afternoon, exploring a breathtaking underwater cave. The cave's intricate formations and the play of light filtering through the water made it feel like an otherworldly cathedral.

We gathered around a crackling bonfire on the beach when the night descended, sharing stories, laughter, and marshmallows toasted to perfection. The waves crashing on the shore provided the soundtrack to our intimate moments.

As the stars painted the night sky, Jensen and I retreated to our cabin on the boat. Wrapped in each other's arms, we watched the moon's reflection dance on the water, grateful for the two days of serenity, adventure, and love we had shared.

Little did we know that our idyllic interlude would soon give way to unexpected challenges. But for those two days, the world was ours, and we basked in the warmth of our love and the beauty of the open sea.

CHAPTER 38

Whatever the reason, Miami traffic has an edge you don't find in other cities. It could be because the relentless sunlight makes everyone yearn for a beachside escape instead of crawling along the busy streets to a tedious job. But on this particular morning, after a blissful weekend, I was determined not to let anything spoil my well-being.

"Good morning, Liv," chirped John as soon as I got inside. "Did you have a lovely weekend?"

"Good morning," I answered, my cheery greeting masking the bombshell I was about to drop on him regarding my relationship with Jensen.

As I recounted my weekend, our phones vibrated, heralding a grim turn of events. A dead man had been found on the beach.

"Goddamn it," Moretti exclaimed, emerging from his office. "This is not what I want on a Monday morning. I want you to go down there and double-check every detail. I want full forensic deployment. Go. I'll monitor the press."

With flashing lights and sirens piercing the morning air, we navigated the homicidal traffic toward our destination,

Nixon Sandbar Marina, on Biscayne Bay.

The tension on the scene was palpable, and for good reason: Miami's marinas weren't typically venues for public displays of violence, and it wasn't easy to believe somebody could get away with it.

The victim was a paramedic; his life abruptly ended with a brutal cut that nearly severed his head. A vacationing couple from Boston stumbled upon the gruesome sight as they disembarked from their boat for an early morning stroll. The amount of blood in the sand indicated the murder had occurred right where the body had been found.

My gaze lingered on the body, an eerie thought creeping in; the wounds resembled those inflicted by the infamous Wilson brothers. Could there be a copycat already at work?

I watched as Tom Bishop and Philippe Balu meticulously combed the area, searching for any trace of evidence.

"What can you tell me, Philippe?" I inquired.

Philippe hesitated for a moment.

"Well, this is only a guess, but I think it's a perfect copycat inspired by the Wilson brothers' crimes."

"My thought exactly," Tom chimed in. "If I didn't know they're in prison, I'd say one of them committed the crime."

They both confirmed what I had also thought.

"Except this time, we have everything we need to identify the criminal: fingerprints, skin, hair," Philippe added.

"And blood," Tom concluded. "The killer is indeed injured."

Their enthusiasm was both encouraging and unsettling.

"Excellent," I said, my mind racing with the implications.

"Nobody saw anything, yet this is one of the most crowded public areas in the city," said one of the officers joining us. "It is impossible just to pop up, kill a guy, and drive away. What do you think, Detective?"

I had my suspicions but didn't want to reveal them.

"Even if somebody saw something, maybe they decided not to report it because they were afraid it would make them a target," I answered.

"Somebody saw something," he persisted, his frustration evident. "Had to."

As the officer walked away to confront a nosy reporter, I spotted John kneeling beside the victim, deep sadness on his face.

"You okay, John?" I asked, concerned.

"I know this man," he replied. "His name is Ambrosio. He lives in my neighbourhood. I'd see him and his mother walk past my house every once in a while."

"I'm sorry, John, but we must keep working to find out who did this to him."

"No. I have to be the one who will give the news to the victim's family. I don't want an officer to give them the news and leave them without answers. I must stay with them and help them through that initial stage somehow."

John's emotional plea touched me, and I agreed, planning to request backup from Maria and Michael. But John was quicker than me.

"I'll request that Maria and Michael back you up," he concluded.

"Could you tell them they'll find me in the marina? There's a good chance the killer is hiding in one of the boats."

"Will do."

I walked away toward the marina. The unforgiving Miami sun blazed overhead as I adopted a casual demeanour, scanning the marina for any sign of the elusive killer. People dressed in shorts and flip-flops passed me, unaware that a murderer was on the loose.

My hope dwindled until I spotted a tiny trail of blood near a boat named Albatross. My instincts overrode any concerns about privacy or warrants. The possibilities swirled in my mind; the killer was hiding on the boat, its owners could be accomplices, or they might be prisoners or casualties. That's when my phone started ringing—the message was overwhelming. Robert Wilson had escaped from prison. It was clear to me now that he was the one who had killed the paramedic.

With my gun drawn, I ventured onto the boat, each step shrouded in silence. As I entered the first cabin, a horrifying scene met my eyes; a man and a woman lay lifeless, blood staining the floor.

I steeled myself to open the next door when a cloth clamped over my mouth, powerful hands pushing me into darkness, and my vision faded as I lost consciousness. The hunt for the killer took an unexpected twist, with me becoming the prey.

The first thing I saw when I regained consciousness was Robert Wilson looking at me with a big smile. My hands and legs were bound with a rope, and I felt a dreadful pain in my head.

"Hello, Liv," he sneered. "Did you miss me? Because I certainly missed you. Do you have any idea how long I've dreamt of this moment? The pleasure I feel to have you at my mercy, finally?"

"The pleasure is all yours," I retorted, frantically searching for a way to free myself.

"As it was yours when you questioned me."

"It has never been a pleasure to see you. Scumbags like you make me puke."

"But you sought me out. And now, you must pay for what you've done. I must make you pay for what you put my mother through."

To keep him talking and buy me some time, I asked, "Why do you revel in causing pain to others?"

"I don't revel in it," he replied coldly. "I exist on a plane of intensity that you and others of your kind can't comprehend. You'll never know the almost god-like power I feel when that last breath escapes a body. It's a sensation of absolute control."

"I understand that feeling of empowerment, the sense of invincibility," I said, trying to reason with him. "But it's an addiction like any other. An addiction that consumes you."

"Oh! Why did I ever think you were more sensitive than the average mortal!" he scoffed. "You're just like them, albeit gorgeous, with skin I've always longed to touch."

He produced a scalpel from his pocket and advanced toward me. I heard myself sigh heavily and wondered if this was how it all would end: killed by a sadistic psychopath.

"This is going to be fun," he sneered, shivering with anticipation, an ugly smile distorting his facial features.

I took a deep breath and tried to wrestle down the panic. I winced as the blade cut deep, blood trickling down my sleeve. Waiting for the right moment, I suddenly curled into a ball, using all the strength in my legs to propel his body into the wall. The sickening sound of bones cracking echoed as he crashed to the floor.

With his scalpel within my reach, I quickly cut the rope that bound me and secured him with a cord length, ensuring he couldn't escape.

My strength waned when I exited the boat to call for help, and I collapsed on the deck. My last conscious thought was to address my wound, as I could feel myself losing too much blood.

CHAPTER 39

I woke up with a pounding headache and a disoriented sense of time and place. The room was filled with beeping machines and spinning contraptions, making it clear that I had landed in a hospital.

As if on cue, a nurse poked her head through the door, her eyes scanning the room's dizzying array of dials and gadgets. She offered me a reassuring smile.

"How are you feeling, Detective Olsen?"

I rubbed my temples and replied, "Apart from this throbbing headache, I feel surprisingly okay."

At that moment, Jensen walked into the room with a concerned face and a steaming cup of coffee. He looked at me with genuine worry.

"Is she all right?" he asked the nurse.

The nurse assured him, "She's fine. I'll go and get the doctor. He can give you more details."

"Did they catch Robert Wilson?" I asked, impatience seeped into my voice.

"They did. Thanks to you," Jensen replied with a mysterious twinkle in his eye.

"How did you even know I was here?" I inquired, curiosity piqued.

Jensen leaned against the doorframe, sipping his coffee.

"John called me. He was here all the time, with your boss and your team members. They only left when the doctor assured them you'd be okay."

"I want to go home. Can you please help me get out of here?"

He eyed me skeptically.

"You're sure you're fine?"

"All I need is a change of clothes and a shower. I'm just a little stiff and sore, that's all," I asserted with determination.

Just as I prepared to rise from the bed, the doctor entered. He greeted us with a friendly smile and then got down to business. He peeled back my eyelid with practiced care and shone a small flashlight into my eyeball.

"Her condition is good," he declared.

"Can she leave the hospital, Doctor?" Jensen asked.

The doctor nodded, his expression thoughtful.

"Yes, she can. However, I do have to warn you. She lost significant blood, so she'll need plenty of rest and nourishment for the next few days."

"Thank you, Doctor," I said, relieved and eager to escape the confines of the hospital and return to the familiar comforts of home.

Less than an hour later, I was lying comfortably on Jensen's sofa, and a delicious aroma wafted from the plate Jensen had placed in front of me on the small table.

"I feel guilty that I didn't find the time to look for Briana Cooper's killer," Jensen declared. These sadistic psychopaths are dangerous; he could have killed you."

"I'm a big girl; I know how to protect myself."

"I see. But I wonder how you did it."

"I was trained to protect myself against guys like him."

"I know detectives get good training, but still. One of the most essential features of the sadistic psychopath is that he is strikingly sure of himself in a confrontation with his victim. That gives him an advantage."

"I wasn't talking about the training we acquire as a detective."

"What's that supposed to mean?"

I hesitated for a while but decided it was time he knew more about me.

"When I was seven, my sister and I witnessed a murder. A twelve-year-old girl was raped and beaten to death before our very eyes. We managed to hide so the perpetrator hadn't seen us. For a long time, we had nightmares, but thanks to our testimony, the culprit received a life sentence."

"Weren't you afraid to testify?"

"Not really. My parents were more scared than we were. Especially after one of the criminals simulated during our testimony that he would slit my sister's and my throat. As a result, my father became almost paranoid and decided to put us into an intensive combat sports training program. He wanted us to learn how to protect ourselves if the opponent was stronger than us. He spent a fortune on the very best trainers. We were training ourselves while our schoolmates took piano, ballet, and the like.

"We grew to love it and started looking for gyms specializing in boxing, MMA, and any sport that could help develop our skills."

"Now I understand. Still having the nightmares?"

"Our nightmares are long gone. But we've gotten into the habit of calling each other regularly and answering whatever the circumstances. If we find it impossible to answer, we'll send a text saying 'I'm okay.'"

"That means you have a great connection as sisters. This does not apply to all siblings."

"I know."

"What did your dad do?"

"He worked for the FBI. But that's enough about me. You must tell me more about yourself now that you know more about me. What about your family?"

"There isn't much to tell. I have a brother. He's a lawyer. We get along well, but we're very different."

"What about your parents?"

"My mother was a history teacher, and my father a lawyer. I always got along with my mother but never with my father."

"Why?"

"My father had built a successful law firm, and there was always this weight of expectation on my shoulders. He always wanted me to follow in his footsteps and was disappointed I didn't."

"Was it because you didn't like being a lawyer?"

"Not really. But that's a long story, and you must be tired. Tonight, you must rest."

"I'm not tired. Don't you think it's time I knew more about you?"

He hesitated momentarily, looking out the window at the faint moonlight.

"It's not that I didn't like the idea of being a lawyer," he began, choosing his words carefully. "It's just that I always felt a calling to something different. Something that wasn't preordained for me by my family. And then, when my brother got into law school, it only heightened the pressure."

"How'd you end up serving?"

"My dad and I clashed one day. He made it clear that as long as I lived under his roof and he covered my expenses, I'd have to follow his rules. Out of sheer rebellion, I decided to enlist. However, being underaged, I needed parental consent. Unexpectedly, my father gave his approval right away. I later found out my mom persuaded him, thinking I'd regret it and come home. But she misjudged. After extensive training and dedication, I was recruited into one of the CIA's elite units."

"And does your father have any idea what you're doing?"

"He's aware I'm not just another grunt, but he doesn't know the specifics."

"Do you still keep in touch?"

"We do. We've made a pact to come together for birthdays and Christmas."

"And your brother?"

"He settled down with a colleague from his law firm and now has two kids. With my dad looking at retirement, he's next in line to run the business. He's the only family who's privy to the nature of my job."

"He's older than you?"

"By three years. But let's save the rest for later. You should rest now."

Held securely in his embrace, I drifted off, his comforting presence enveloping me.

For the next few days, I was lulled into total happiness. I had no idea that my joy would be short-lived and that the following events would turn my life upside down for years.

CHAPTER 40

On a bright Thursday morning, with the sun already high in the sky and traffic bustling, I returned to the office. Upon entering headquarters, a wave of compliments greeted me.

"You're truly exceptional at what you do," remarked Maria.

"I consider myself fortunate to work alongside someone of your calibre," Michael said.

"I couldn't agree more," John added with a smirk. "You're one incredible detective."

I felt a little embarrassed by so many compliments.

"The credit goes to the amazing team I have by my side," I said. "Speaking of which, anyone up for a cup of coffee?" I added, eager to change the topic.

"On it," John replied.

Maria raised her hand playfully, "What about me? Mind making one for me, too?"

"Of course! How do you take yours?" John asked.

She winked, "Black and strong, just like you."

We all burst into laughter, and I felt welcome for the first time since I'd worked here.

The media frenzy that Robert Wilson's capture generated was more extensive than anticipated, and without knowing it, I had become a star. During my few days at his place, Jensen didn't let me watch the news, and I wasn't aware of it. "Relax," he was saying. "Take some time just for yourself … with me," he added with a mischievous grin.

I don't know how the reporters found out so quickly that I was back at work, but I was deluged with interview requests. I turned down the interviews without showing them any actual hostility. But the attention continued; everyone at headquarters stopped me to say nice things, shake my hand, and tell me what a good job I had done.

After the initial shock subsided, I inquired about how Robert Wilson had evaded prison confinement.

"The corrections officers discovered him lying on the ground, frothing at the mouth," John explained. "After a detailed examination in the prison medical wing, it was found that he had advanced stomach cancer. The decision was made to transfer him to a specialist hospital. However, during the ambulance ride there, he overpowered the two officers with him and coerced the paramedic to alter the route. The rest, as you are aware, is history. He killed three other innocents."

"That's what killers do. They need it, just like the rest of us need air," I said.

None of us said anything for a long time; we were lost in our thoughts. I had just finished my coffee when Moretti appeared.

"Detective Olsen! I wasn't expecting you back at work so soon. How are you feeling?"

"Good, thank you, Sergeant. I'm rested and in great shape."

"Thank God. We had some emotions. I hope Mr. Hunt

told you we were all present at the hospital to wait for the doctor's verdict."

"He did."

"By the way, I like him. He's a good match for you."

"Thank you, Sergeant."

"I remind you that there's still paperwork to be done. But first, there is something more pressing we need to address."

"What could be more pressing?"

He motioned for John and me to follow him.

Curiosity piqued, we trailed behind, uncertain of what awaited us. Moretti's grave demeanour hinted it was no ordinary debrief.

"As you're now aware, Robert Wilson is in the last stages of cancer. Because of that, he decided to come clean about every sin he's committed."

"So, countless families will finally get their closure. It's a good thing," I said with a mixture of relief and shock.

"But," Moretti hesitated, "he's made a rather specific demand."

"Which is?" I asked.

"He's only going to confess to you, Detective Olsen,"

"Sergeant, you can't possibly expect Liv to confront that monster again!" interjected John immediately. "Not after everything he's put her through!"

"I share your sentiments, Detective Freeman," Moretti said, nodding in understanding. "It's why I'm leaving the decision in Detective Olsen's hands."

"I'll face him," I said without hesitation. "Wilson's mind games never fazed me," I added, drawing a deep breath.

Moretti studied me for a moment.

"You're certain about this?" he asked.

I nodded. "My choice is made."

"Fine," he sighed. "But, Detective Freeman, you're accompanying her."

"Wouldn't have it any other way," John responded with grim determination.

"All right, then," nodded Moretti. "I'll arrange everything and keep you both posted."

Halfway through my third cup of coffee, Moretti told me it was time. Sooner than anticipated, but I was eager to confront this final challenge.

I drank my last sip of coffee and signalled to John that it was time to go. The morning rush hour was dying down, and the traffic moved quickly enough all the way to the prison.

We showed our credentials and followed the corrections officer through several corridors. To my surprise, we found Robert Wilson inside the prison infirmary.

"Liv … it is so good to see you," he exclaimed, his voice wanting to appear tender. "Come closer. There is so much to tell … and so little time."

"What is he doing in the jail infirmary?" I asked, furious to find him there.

"Those are the orders, Detective!" answered one of the corrections officers in charge.

"He killed so many people! He's supposed to be in a maximum-security unit!"

"He's receiving treatment for cancer," explained the officer.

"You're moving him back and forth when you know full well he's smart enough to escape again!"

"Even prisoners are entitled to medical care, Detective," the officer added.

"He's not a regular prisoner. He's a monster."

"C'mon, Liv," intervened Robert Wilson in a voice meant to sound gentle. "We've been through a lot together, you and I. And I feel we'd gotten to know each other pretty well. You don't have any pity?"

"Oh! Shut up! Do you expect emotions when you don't

have any? Why don't you tell these people what you enjoy doing the most?"

"Now, Liv. You know that's too private, even between us. Come closer," he said in a hoarse voice.

"Don't listen to him, Liv," said John. "Don't get close."

"Don't you want to hear something very, very bad that I did, Liv? You wouldn't want me to die before I tell you, would you?" Robert Wilson said, looking at me with his awful, frozen smile.

"Please keep your distance, Detective," said one of the corrections officers, starting to understand that Robert Wilson was not a regular criminal.

"Nobody knows everything, Liv … nobody knows, but I'll tell you. Only you," continued Robert Wilson, ignoring the officer's intervention.

"What about my partner?" I asked him.

"I don't like Blacks. They smell bad. Get him out of here. But you … you smell like wildflowers in the spring."

I knew there was no other way to get answers than to comply with his demands.

"John! Wait for me outside."

"But…"

"Please," I insisted.

I turned around and pushed the record button on my phone without Robert Wilson seeing me. He hadn't agreed to have his confession recorded.

"All right," I said. "Start talking."

"Tell me, Liv, do you remember what you wanted when you were fourteen?"

"What does that have to do with me? You said you want to tell me something that nobody knows. What's that?"

"Oh! I will tell you. At fourteen, I had my first kill, a sweet girl from my neighbourhood. I remember the look in her eyes: so hurt, confused and desperate. And my hand feeling so steady with the scalpel, moving up and arching back for a perfect cut."

"Can you tell me who she was?" I asked, trying to keep calm.

"What does it matter what her name was? She's gone now."

"If you are unwilling to confess, I'm leaving," I said, standing up and heading for the door.

"No, don't leave. I'll tell you everything."

For two hours, his words cascaded in an unabated waterfall of malice, unmasking buried deeds that had slumbered in the catacombs of his consciousness. Jacksonville, New York, Miami—each city, a chapter of orchestrated crimes with deliberate and sadistic precision, performed by minds where empathy had long since decayed. It all came pouring out of him.

"Have you ever felt any remorse?" I asked.

"Remorse?" He parroted an eerie calmness emanating from his voice. "Perhaps, initially, when we became accomplices to our mother's murderous escapades. But the electrifying thrill, the omnipotent rush, eclipsed any flicker of conscience. Resistance was futile."

As I pondered whether malevolence could be genetic, the image of Nancy Connery, the matriarch of malice, flickered through my mind. The woman who birthed two monsters drowned their humanity in a toxic swamp of cruelty and chaos.

"Can I delve into some personal questions?" I gently probed.

His gaze, a perplexing amalgamation of faux tenderness and concealed malice, settled on me.

"I don't mind. A few more moments bathing in your scent won't hurt. Fire away."

Disgust knotted in my stomach, but it was imprisoned

behind a stoic demeanour essential for extracting truths.

"At what age did your mother reveal herself to you?"

"I was six. But the revelation of her maternal link came only years later."

"And how did she infiltrate your life?"

He detailed an intricate web of manipulation, where, after six years, Nancy Connery became an invaluable asset to the orphanage, slithering her way into their lives through the porous defences of their adoptive parents.

"They could have sought help. Reported her," I probed.

"They could've," he agreed calmly. "But the fear of losing us and the fear of her retribution choked their resistance. She'd promised a fate worse than death if they intervened. They submissively acquiesced when faced with her genuine efforts toward orphan welfare."

"If not for your mother, your adoptive parents might still breathe, and your life could have been different."

My statement was accusatory, yet factual.

"You have no jurisdiction over my mother's narrative," he bristled, an unbridled fury flickering momentarily. "She graced us with profoundly exhilarating moments that mere mortals like you could never fathom."

Swallowing the abrasive retort dancing on my tongue, I opted for strategic silence, unwilling to jeopardize the delicate bridge to his revelations.

"Did Mr. Harry Miller know of his kinship with you?"

"Mother ensured he knew," he said, a sinister smirk tracing his lips. "Becoming his company lawyer, freshly graduated, was not luck. Our concealed threats haunted his daily existence, terrified that we'd obliterate his family and reputation."

"But his suffering wasn't enough."

"No. His demise was a meticulous masterpiece, a drawn-out symphony of agony that ended with his pleas for merciful death."

"You've never regretted the innocent lives obliterated by your hands?"

"Never. Yet, there resides one regret."

His voice was cold, unyielding.

"And that is?"

"That I couldn't engrave my signature onto your pristine skin, disassembling your form into grotesque art."

"And you never will. Your days are numbered," I said as I vacated the room, my voice steady, unshaken.

Despite the bitter taste lingering in my mouth, I exhaled, reconciling with the haunting dance of confronting malice incarnate.

CHAPTER 41

Y ou look very pale," said John, who was waiting for me by the door, ready to intervene if Robert Wilson didn't behave.

"Well, I've always believed that there's good in everyone, even the most inveterate criminals. But this one is pure evil. I'm glad he won't be part of this world for long.

"Did he confess to everything?"

"He did."

"Congratulations, partner," he said, slapping me on the shoulder.

I turned my phone off and headed toward the car. John said nothing on our way back to headquarters, and I was grateful for his silence. I needed some time with myself to shake off the bitter feeling that meeting Robert Wilson had left.

We found Moretti in his office. He closed a file on his desk and looked up, surprised.

"You're done? Already? Well?" he asked.

I placed my phone on the desk before him and settled onto the edge of a chair. He began listening to the recording, frowning at each confession, nodding occasionally, and making notes. Sometimes, he stopped the recording to ask me questions.

I found it hard to sit still and listen to Robert Wilson's confession again. I wanted it to end and never hear his voice again.

Silence settled over the office when the recording stopped, and I thought that a toxic air of malice floated through the air. Finally, Moretti stood up, came around the desk, and shook my hand.

"This is just terrific, Liv. Great job."

His handshake was firm, dry, and manly; this was the first time he'd used my first name.

"I'll notify Jacksonville and New York to reopen the files," he said. "All the families of the people involved will finally find peace. And once you finish writing the report, we can close this chapter for good."

I wasn't thrilled about writing my report, but it was a task I couldn't avoid. I hadn't eaten anything all day, and the copious amounts of coffee I had consumed had left me feeling saturated. I slumped at my desk and began to write, eager to complete the task and escape the nightmarish world into which Robert Wilson had thrust me. My relief was palpable when my phone rang, and Jensen's voice whispered in my ear. "Hello, Liv. How was your day?"

"Terrible."

"Don't fret about it. I have something that will take your mind off everything. I've got a surprise for you."

"What kind of surprise?"

"This weekend, I'll whisk you away on an adventure."

"I adore adventures," I replied, my voice filled with excitement.

"Then wrap up your work and come over. Dinner is almost ready." His voice was soothing and gentle, instantly erasing the day's horrors from my mind. I completed my report and rushed out of the office. I was halfway to Jensen's apartment when my phone chimed with a message from him.

I'm sorry, Liv, but something urgent has come up, and I must leave town. It might be a while before I return. I'll explain everything as soon as I can. Love you, Jensen.

I tried to remain optimistic, convincing myself he must have had a valid reason for cancelling our plans. Perhaps a pressing case required his attention, and he needed to act quickly. If I hurried, I might catch him before he left.

After navigating through traffic for an eternity, I arrived at the parking lot of Jensen's building. I was about to leave the car when I saw Jensen emerging from the front door, accompanied by a beautiful brunette holding a young child's hand. My heart sank as I watched the woman rest her head on his chest, and he wrapped his arms around her shoulders. They stood like that for a while before getting into Jensen's car and driving away from the parking lot.

The world stopped momentarily, and a sudden, icy chill rolled through my body. The only explanation was that this woman was his ex-wife, whom he had never told me about, who had his child, and he had chosen her over me.

I remained frozen, overwhelmed by the pain in my heart. I had allowed myself to be captivated by his charm, intoxicated by the intensity of our relationship, unafraid to acknowledge my feelings. And now, he had shattered my heart into pieces.

That night, I couldn't sleep. As soon as the first rays of the sun rose over the city, I left the house. I ran for miles, swam, and kicked a punching ball in the gym until I was exhausted. On Sunday evening, my sister called to inform me that she would be in Miami for a fashion show in two weeks.

"And guess who's joining us?" she said. "David. After all this time, he's still head over heels for you. I told him it's an obsession."

"See you in two weeks, Sis," I replied, choosing not to comment on David. Our relationship had been brief, and we had parted as friends.

When I drove to work Monday morning, I was still trying to figure out how to navigate the days ahead, feeling completely emotionless.

"Good morning, Liv," said John cheerfully. "Are you going to ask for a vacation?"

"And why would I do that?"

"Well, my brother told me that he and Jensen would close the agency for a while because they need a vacation. I thought you'd be off with Jensen somewhere. It'll be good for you after all the stress you've been under."

"Has your brother decided where to go?" I asked, channelling the discussion in another direction.

"He's already gone. All he said was that he wanted to show his wife the world."

Just as Jensen wanted to do, I thought. *Show his wife the world.*

"Sorry, John, but I desperately need a cup of coffee," I said, seeking a reason to end the conversation.

I had time to take a few steps toward the coffee machine when the phone rang; someone had been shot dead. I got into the daily routine, and life went on.

Jensen hasn't contacted me since the day he left. It became clear that everything between us meant nothing to him.

Days blended into weeks. It was a lifeless existence, and the torment I felt inside was almost more than I could bear, a torture worse than anything I'd ever felt.

When my sister arrived, I realized how much I'd missed her. We'd always been very close, sharing every secret and being there for each other. We stayed up all night, and I told her all about Jensen. She shared my happy moments and wept with me for my pain.

"You have experienced something very uncommon with Jensen," she said. "Most people long their whole lives for something like that. And never feel it."

"I know that. But no one wants to feel my pain right now."

"I think it's time for you to come home. I understand you've needed time to heal after mom's death. It was the same reason I managed to model in Europe, to be away from places that stirred up painful memories. But you're alone here. You have all your friends and relatives in New York, and you have me. Promise me you'll think about it."

"I'll think about it. I promise."

That evening, she forced me to wear one of her gorgeous dresses and attend the fashion show. David and the girls were all delighted to see me. The fashion show was successful, and the party continued until the early morning. I felt like I was among friends for the first time since my arrival in Miami.

That night, I couldn't help but ponder my sister's advice. It may be time to return home to New York, where my friends and relatives waited.

A month later, I made a difficult decision and resigned. It was sad to part with my team members, but the call to return home was too strong. I closed the apartment and headed for the airport.

As I gazed out the plane window, taking one last look at the sea, I had a vision; I saw the outline of Jensen's strong shape looming in the reddish light of the sunset. And in that moment, I knew I'd never love anyone like I loved him.

Deep down inside, without wanting to acknowledge it, I couldn't help but wonder if fate might bring us together again someday.

9 781738 329601